Love Thy Neighbor

Love
Thy
Neighbor

By Diane Moore

Parson Place Press
Mobile, Alabama

Love Thy Neighbor is a work of fiction. Other than places referred to for purposes incidental to the plot, all of the names, characters, places and events that appear in the book are the product of the author's imagination. Any resemblance to actual events, locales or persons, living or dead, is entirely coincidental.

Cover and interior design and layout by Just Ink Digital Design.

ISBN: 978-0-9842163-7-6

Library of Congress Control Number: 2012933358

Acknowledgements

I want to thank God and the promptings of the Holy Spirit for making this book a reality. He lined my path with wonderful people and opportunities that guided me to stay on course.

Special thanks to my husband, Pat, who spent countless hours reading, editing, and putting witty words into my characters' minds and mouths, to keep me and now you the readers entertained. His devotion to and love for me are blessings.

To my awesome sons Barclay and Jake, who began this journey with me when they were mere babes, learning to live with my writing habits. To my wonderful daughters Erika and Andrea who let me bounce ideas off of them when they often had no idea what I was talking about. To my lovely daughters-in-law, Erin and Amanda, and beautiful stepchildren, Erin, Raleigh, Chris, and Cassie, who humor me with tolerance and patience as I share the trials and tribulations of my characters.

To my friend and first editor Lauri Gray Eaton, who always made my writing better and taught me to keep it concise. Thank you to Grand Master Kim, Mrs. Kim and the instructors and students at Kim's Tae Kwon Do Academy who taught me the true value of integrity. To my friends at Valero Energy Corp. and VeloValero Bike team who have been an inspiration and great support.

A special thank you to my writing critique groups – the San Antonio Christian Writer's Group and San Antonio Romance Authors. And thank yous to publisher Michael White and Parson Place Press for believing in the story, and to Elaine and Just Ink Digital for the wonderful cover and interior design.

CHAPTER ONE

His eyes remained open, but the rest of his body had shut down. Blood pulsed, then trickled down the front of his throat, crawling into the cavity just short of his collarbone, where it formed a shallow reservoir.

She watched and was intrigued at how the color of his blood strongly resembled the deep color of the 2000 Barolo, a bold Northern Italian wine, they had just finished drinking together.

She followed the narrow streams of fluid as they began to crawl down toward his chest. She thought they looked like slender fingers reaching for his chest hairs, grasping for survival. The vibrant color of Jimmy Lee Hayden's blood dulled as he sank into lifelessness.

The knife in his throat assured his silence ... forever.

"You'll never tell my secrets," she said to him, and then she turned to walk away, dropping a gold necklace on her retreat.

She grasped the doorknob. Her hands were covered with three layers of latex gloves. *Insurance in case one or two ripped. The gloves were fragile. Like life.*

She locked the door from the inside and closed it slowly behind her. *Now, off to work.*

* * *

Detective Stuart Beaumont arrived at the San Antonio Police Department's downtown headquarters at 6 a.m. He liked arriving at his office before the 7:15 a.m. shift change for two reasons. First, it was quiet for about 30 minutes, which allowed him to gather his thoughts. Second, he could catch-up with officers as they arrived back in from the 3rd shift. That way, he knew what cases might still be lingering from the night before. Stuart sipped Ginseng tea while he read through the most recent files.

"Shooting, shooting, knife, knife, shooting, knife, domestic ... what's this?" He pulled out the report from the neatly stacked pile on his desk and began reading more intently. "A knife in the throat, through the Adam's Apple. Sounds like the return of Bruce Lee."

His eyes rested on the name, "Jimmy Lee Hayden." As he continued reading, the facts fell into place. Stuart shifted in his chair. "Not her again."

Stuart slammed his finger onto the intercom button.

The voice on the other end of the intercom said, "Detective Roberts."

"Hey, Mike," Stuart said. "Come in here. I believe we've got a 'hot' one."

"What's up, L.G.?" Stuart smiled at the shortened version of his nickname. In his early days on the force, the squad began calling him Lucky Guy, for surviving many near-death incidents that happened in the line of police duty.

"Look here, Mike," Stuart held up the file. "This murder at 10 Kensington Circle, where the ritzy people move to get away from all of the crime." Stuart tossed the file back onto his desk.

Detective Mike Roberts nodded.

"We got this gal – Morgan's her last name – an *investee-gative* reporter for the San Antonio *Daily Sun* –" he mis-pronounced deliberately as he opened up and read from the file. "She lives next door to the victim. I don't want to see her sensationalizing this case in the news. We'll end up spending more time answering media calls and holding press confer-ences than investigating the murder." Stuart thumbed through the papers in the file.

"I think she'll stay away from this one, L.G." Mike looked around the room. He casually stood and walked to the file cabinet located on the side wall of Stuart's office, where water bottles were lined up neatly along the top. Mike moved towards them, grabbed one water bottle and then held up another, offering it to Stuart.

"Why's that?" Stuart shook his head and held his hand in front of him, signaling that he didn't want the water.

"Take a sip of that golden tea and read on." Mike smiled and made himself comfortable in the classroom-style wooden chair.

Stuart continued reading. He stopped and looked up at Mike. "We're considering her as a person of interest? Give me the skinny."

"We're questioning her this morning." Mike put down his water, reached for the koosh ball on Stuart's desk and tossed it up and down, back and forth to each hand.

"As a possible eyewitness only, right?" Stuart snatched the ball mid-air from Mike. "I don't want any police harassment cases printed in tomorrow's paper." Stuart squished the ball and then flung it up in the air, the rubbery strands soft against his palm. "These pushy reporters. You mark my words, Mike, we'll bring her in for questioning and the next thing you know, *she'll* be asking all the questions – interviewing our officers ... I think I'd better handle this one myself."

Stuart picked up the file folder again, shuffled through some papers and focused on the D.O.B. "Twenty-eight years old – too young to be messing with this kind of case." He threw the ball into the trash can opposite the wall from his desk. "That's also pretty young to have a house in that area of town, don't you think?"

"It's a nice area. Maybe she does well. I learned that she moved down here from the Midwest." Mike retrieved the ball from the trash can. "Maybe she struck it rich up there, and then decided to come to God's country – Texas." Mike smiled and then cleared his throat. "Seriously, L.G., I know you have this love-hate relationship with news types." Mike said as he tossed the koosh ball towards the trash can.

"They're all just trying to win the next Pulitzer." Stuart watched as the blue and red ball strands stuck on the trash can's rim. "They don't think about how they might jeopardize our investigation." Stuart shook his head, pushed back in his chair, rose and strode towards the trash can. "Or, they just don't think." He loosened the koosh ball from the trash can rim, squeezed it and carried it back to his desk.

Mike shifted in his chair. "Like I said, two officers are headed there this morning. We'll get Ms. Morgan's statement as a possible eyewitness and we'll go from there." Mike set down the water and wrung his hands as he looked toward the door.

"Okay. Let me know their ETA. I'll drop by her house just after they arrive."

Mike stood to leave.

"Hey," Stuart looked at the ball and then toward the trash can. "Between you and me, Mike, I'm not going to have another dead journalist on my conscience." With little effort, Stuart gracefully shot the koosh ball into the trash can. "And this Deirdre Morgan. We've had our run-ins before."

* * *

"Deirdre Morgan?" the aged and plump policeman addressed the stylishly dressed young woman. *Officer Buffet,* Deirdre thought, as he leaned casually against the corner pillar of her front porch.

Deirdre stood in the open doorway of her two-story colonial brick home. She squinted to block the morning sun's glare, allowing her to focus on Officer Buffet and glance at a younger officer who stood beside him.

"What has my neighbor dragged me into now?" Deirdre resented the intrusion.

The older officer stepped forward. "Do you mind if we come in and ask you a few questions?"

Deirdre opened the door wider and gestured for the officers to enter. "Come on in. I've got a few minutes." She turned and led them toward the kitchen.

"Not working today?" Officer Buffet asked as Deirdre motioned for the officers to sit at the mahogany, sleek-lined, kitchen table.

As one of the city newspaper's top investigative reporters, Deirdre often worked closely with law enforcement officials, but this didn't seem like a social visit, and she didn't have time to compare notes on local events.

"Actually, I'm taking care of some legal business. At 9:30 this morning, I'm meeting with lawyers downtown," she responded. "You remember, Go-Green Landscapers ran over and killed my neighbor Letty's dog." Deirdre crossed her arms. "After they left her fence gate open."

"Oh, yes, that," the older officer frowned and met her gaze.

Deirdre remembered. He had taken the initial police report.

"Go-Green Landscapers has been the city's preferred landscaper for years." Officer Buffet clasped his hands together and rested them on the table.

Deirdre remained unmoved.

Officer Buffet then unclasped his hands and leaned back in his chair. "That's just like you, Miss Morgan, to go out on a limb for a friend."

Deirdre moved gracefully into her chair. "It's the right thing to do." She fidgeted with her blouse sleeve. "To tell the truth."

Officer Buffet crossed his arms, scanned Deirdre suspiciously, and nodded.

The younger officer curtly tapped his foot on the Oriental rug that covered Deirdre's hardwood floors. He seemed nervous.

Stretch, Deirdre thought. *He looks like an over-grown Gumby doll.*

Officer Buffet cleared his throat and leaned forward in his chair. "We're not going to take much of your time, *Ms.* Morgan." He emphasized the "Ms." "We're here on another investigation regarding your neighbor at 10 Kensington Circle." He shifted in his chair, stopped suddenly, glanced at his young partner, and then looked directly at Deirdre and asked: "Did you notice anything or anyone strange in the neighborhood last night or very early this morning?"

Deirdre locked her gaze on Officer Buffet.

"If this is about someone parked in front of my neighbor's house again, I'd rather you not waste my time," Deirdre said. "You and I and the homeowner association's lawyers know that the street is public domain. Anyone can park on it." Deirdre leaned forward in her chair, clasped her hands and rested them on the table, ready to put this issue to rest.

"Well, Ms. Morgan." *Stretch* interrupted this time. "It's not about anything like that."

"We wouldn't waste your time with something petty like that," Officer Buffet addressed her with all the warmth of a loving grandfather. "You see, Ms. Morgan, your next-door neighbor, Jimmy Lee Hayden, was found dead in his home, at 2 a.m. We believe it was a homicide. So, we're questioning all of the neighbors to find out if they saw or heard anything suspicious."

"I can't believe it," Deirdre dropped back into her chair. "I just can't believe it. Who? How?" She looked from one officer to the other, searching their faces for any non-verbal clues.

"We thought you might help us. We knew that you and your neighbor had some ... well," he cleared his throat, "incidents in the past and that there was some animosity between you and Mr. Hayden ..."

A loud knock on the door startled Deirdre. She jumped to her feet, headed toward the door and opened it.

A well-dressed, handsome man stood in Deirdre's doorway. His wavy black hair was so dark that with the reflection of the sunlight beaming in from her doorway, it looked as if it were highlighted with a midnight blue tint. As she scanned his well-cut, more than six-foot frame, her eyes were drawn to the left side of his neatly pressed suit. It was slightly drawn back, exposing a badge marked "DETECTIVE."

Oh, yes, I remember you.

"Deirdre Morgan," his strong voice, which matched his muscular physique, jolted Deirdre's thoughts back to the present. "I'm Head Homicide Detective Stuart Beaumont," he handed her his business card. "May I come in? I see that some of my officers are here, and I need a moment with them."

His eyes reminded her of a vat of dark chocolate, *sweet enough to tempt one to jump in, but dangerous and deceptive.* "Yes, of course." She motioned for him to enter.

With the door still open, Deirdre stepped onto her front porch. Usually, a homicide scene would draw much more attention. In her line of work, she had often followed tips from police scanners; hightailed it directly to a crime scene, arriving alongside or shortly after several other media trucks. But her sleepy suburban street was eerily quiet, considering a homicide had been discovered a few hours ago, and that Head Homicide Detective Beaumont was here. Even the usual barking from her neighbor's dog Princeton was absent. *Strange.*

* * *

Stuart headed toward the two officers, hoping that Deirdre hadn't noticed his slight pause when her near-emerald green eyes met his. He walked past her, breathing in the sophisticated scent of her perfume and noticing how her sunlight-kissed, dusty blond hair glistened.

"Good morning, Detective Beaumont." The officers stood up. Stuart motioned for the officers to sit down. Stuart kept his voice low as he shared some notes and a brief conversation with the officers.

As he closed his notebook, Stuart noticed a photo hanging on the wall behind the table. The photo displayed Deirdre Morgan posing with 9th Degree Black Belt, Grand Master In Mook Kim. A well-known Grand Master in Tae Kwon Do, Kim had schools – or "Do Jangs" as referred to on the TKD circuit – throughout the nation, but he called San Antonio home.

In the photo, Deirdre beamed as she smiled – her petite frame nearly enveloped in her Tae Kwon Do uniform, which the Koreans referred to as a "Do Bak." She was wearing a Black Belt with one yellow stripe, Stuart noted. He would jot that down later. He didn't want to seem obvious right now – too much at stake.

Deirdre stood inside the open doorway. "Is there any more information about my neighbor's death?"

Stuart turned toward the door. "No, Ms. Morgan. Just what these officers told you. That's all we know." Stuart noticed the disappointment in her eyes.

She paused, then perked up. "Has the time of death been determined ..."

"Ms. Morgan." Stuart cut her off. "I apologize for the brisk introduction earlier. I know that you are a seasoned investigative reporter, so I hope that for now this is all off the record."

"As long as I can have an exclusive," Deirdre said.

Reporters. Always seeking the headlines. Wanting to be the first to break the news.

"I'm sure we can work something out. To answer your question though, it's too early to say the exact time of death. As you know, tests have to be done, an autopsy, dusting (for fingerprints). Our forensics team is on top of it." He paused. "I am curious though, and I wonder if I could ask *you* a question."

"Sure." Deirdre crossed her arms in front of her.

"How would you describe your neighbor, Jimmy Lee Hayden?"

Deirdre looked past Stuart and the officers. She glanced in the direction of her neighbor's house and she took a deep breath. She wrinkled her brow and let out a sigh. She slowly raised her head and looked directly at Stuart. The corner of her lips slightly upturned as if she were suppressing a smile. When she spoke, there was a lingering pause between the words. "Dead. White. Male."

The two police officers muffled their chuckles.

Stuart shot them a warning glance. *Cute. She does have a way with words.*

"Let me rephrase my question. How would you describe him *when he was alive*?"

Deirdre relaxed her arms and glanced at her feet. Stuart noticed that her hair fell just above her shoulders. Before she answered his second question, Deirdre loosely clasped her hands in front of her torso. Stuart admired her slender fingers and manicured, red-polished nails. She moistened her perfectly defined lips when she began to speak.

"I'd rather not respond to that until I have more time to think. If you've gone over the police reports from the past, you know that Jimmy Lee Hayden and I had what I would call 'drama.' I really need time to reflect on all of that before I can give you a thoughtful and honest answer," Deirdre said.

CHAPTER TWO

Stuart welcomed the thirty minute drive back to his office. When he arrived at his desk, he pulled out a drawer and reached for his Bible.

> *"Trust in the Lord with all thine heart; and lean not unto thine own understanding." Proverbs 3:5*

Stuart prayed. He heard footsteps and a light knock on the door. He closed his Bible and the drawer.

When he looked up, Detective Roberts was standing in front of him. He had a folder in his hand.

"Seriously L.G., I know you don't particularly care for news types," Mike said as he tossed the folder onto Stuart's desk.

Mike displayed open palms. "But maybe we can use Deirdre's investigative reporting skills *for* us, instead of them working *against* us."

"Are you kidding?" Stuart quipped. "She has her sights set on a headline news story. She's already asked for an exclusive."

Mike's eyes flashed toward the folder. "Have you seen any of her news reports? She has a real eye for detail." Mike grabbed and turned a chair, then straddled it.

"Sounds like you're a real fan, Mike," Stuart studied Mike, and then followed his gaze back to the folder.

"Well, not really." Mike nodded towards the folder. "But the Chief is, and he wants us to work with her, not to shut her out." Mike rested his elbows on the chair's back.

"Oh, c'mon." Stuart shook his head and pushed back in his chair. He couldn't believe what he was hearing. His frustration rose. He stood and began pacing the room. The collar tightened around his neck. "Isn't Chief worried about her leaking clues? Sensationalizing? Editorializing? The Dan Rather-James Brady syndrome? Getting the news first – even if it's incorrect? And if that wasn't enough, then in 2004, Rather turned around and did it again when he didn't confirm President George Bush's military records and broadcast a bogus story about President Bush."

Mike raised his hands and nodded. "Yes, that was curtains for Dan Rather."

"And the Chief isn't worried about that with Deirdre Morgan?"

"Apparently not." Mike shifted in his chair.

Stuart returned to his desk and sat down. His hands rested on the folder.

"I remember exactly where I was when I heard the news about James Brady and President Reagan being shot. A bunch of us were studying in the dorm together when the news bulletin came on the television. At the time, I was going to follow in Dad's footsteps and become a reporter, so it was ironic that Mom called me when she saw the newscast on CBS. I can still remember the sadness in her voice when she heard the news that her acquaintance James Brady was dead. I thought Mom was going to collapse during that telephone call." Stuart's palms were sweaty.

"And to think that everyone in the nation – including his family and friends were hearing the news at the same time from a practical stranger – Dan Rather."

He paused. "Then remember the surgeon's quote after the successful surgery?" Stuart grabbed the koosh ball and tossed it to Mike.

Mike caught the ball. "Wasn't it something like, 'no one informed *us* that my patient, James Brady, was dead.'"

"Right. That was classic. That line is how I'll always remember Dr. Arthur Kobrine." Stuart smiled and then his lips slowly curled downward.

He cradled his head in his hands. Talk of the media and news reporters brought back ghosts from his past.

"I know, L.G." Mike leaned forward in his chair and gently placed the koosh ball on Stuart's desk. Mike got up to get Stuart a bottle of water.

Stuart rubbed his eyes before looking up at Mike. "Thanks." He took the bottle, opened it and took a long drink.

"No problem. You can get beyond this." Mike sat silently.

Stuart nodded and stared at his distorted reflection in the curved bottle of water.

"These news people!" Stuart hammered his clenched fist on top of the file folder on the desk.

Mike and Stuart were interrupted by a light tap on Stuart's door. "Come in."

The department secretary walked into Stuart's office and handed him a folder marked "Physical Evidence."

Mike took the secretary's entrance as his cue to exit.

"Detective Beaumont," the receptionist's voice came over the intercom before he had a chance to open the folder.

"There's a Lucy Menendez on line one. She wants to speak to you about an incident on Kensington Circle. The file should be on your desk."

"Send the call through." After a slight pause, Stuart picked up the telephone receiver. "Detective Beaumont."

"Detective Beaumont, my name is Lucy Menendez. I've got some information you might be interested in." Her words rushed out.

"Princeton, my dog, had to go out last night about midnight. I was letting Princeton in when I heard a sound out front. I looked out my front window and saw a lady run from the side of the Hayden house and across the lawn. It was dark, and I couldn't make out where she went. She could've run anywhere. The only thing I can think of is that she must've run into his neighbor – Deirdre Morgan's house. Now that I'm talking about it and remembering, I think that woman *must've* run into the neighbor's yard. And Deirdre Morgan lives right next door. The lady was the same size as Deirdre Morgan, too – small, a little on the skinny side." She took a deep breath.

"Anyway, Detective Beaumont, many of my neighbors are very upset about this. I called you as soon as I left Mrs. Hayden's house. The neighbors around here and me, we're very worried and we're willing to help out so you can catch the killer right away. This kind of thing doesn't happen in our neighborhood. Not as long as I've been here, and that's over ten years."

Stuart wrote notes as quickly as he could. He knew there'd be a back-up tape of the conversation if he needed it.

"Have you spoken to your neighbors, Ms. Menendez?"

"Yes, most of my neighbors. I know all of them ... well most of them. We are very close and we watch out for each other. We keep an eye on things in the neighborhood for everybody. And we watch Deirdre Morgan. Did you know that she's a single woman, living in a house alone? How does she pay for that house all by herself? She has visitors. Sometimes late at night, sometimes in the middle of the day. And she goes out late at night and sometimes doesn't come home until one or two o'clock in the morning. What's a young woman doing out that late, Detective Beaumont? Isn't that strange? And we know that's true. We've always watched her."

"I see," Stuart said, smiling to himself. After a slight pause, he asked, "Did you telephone the police last night or, umm, early this morning, when you saw this strange person running across the yard?" Stuart turned to his computer and was already checking the 9-1-1 telephone log.

"Well, no. I thought maybe Deirdre Morgan was having some of her friends over again. You know she does that. She has friends over, *all kinds* of friends that we don't know."

Stuart tapped his pencil on the folder, which sat atop papers piled on his desk. Ms. Menendez – or someone for whom she was a mouthpiece – had set opinions about Deirdre Morgan, he thought.

"Ms. Menendez, did you tell anyone else about this incident?"

"No." She hesitated. "I called you right away."

"Good. I'm glad you did. Would you be available sometime this morning or maybe later today for me to stop by, visit, and take your statement? Or, if you'd prefer, you can come down to the station – in case you think the neighbors would be suspicious, or if it might cause your neighbors to talk."

"Sure, I'll be here. Let me talk to my husband to see what he wants to do. Can I call you right back?"

"Absolutely," Stuart said. "I'll wait for your call." Stuart hung up the phone and opened the folder marked "Physical Evidence," and, with self-satisfaction, said to himself, "I think I'll be able to convince the Chief by the end of the day that Deirdre Morgan's involvement in this case is definitely a conflict of interest."

CHAPTER THREE

Deirdre adjusted the collar of her white silk blouse. Her sweat beaded underneath it. Her fingers grasped the cool stem of her *lucky* pen. She glanced down, then placed the pen on the edge of the *Daily Sun's* executive conference room table.

"What you're telling me is that the city housing authority hired this security company, Rightway Security, to guard the housing project. Rightway does the drug busts, confiscates the drugs and then resells them back on the street," Joe Brown, the managing editor of the *Daily Sun*, summarized Deirdre's news report, while the buttons across his belly strained to keep his shirt together.

Big lunch at La Fonda.

Deirdre, Joe, Marcy Cavarino, the *Daily's Sun's* lead attorney, and Curtis Green, one of the *Sun's* top photographers, were seated at the round table in the conference room. The door was closed. Joe and Marcy had full mugs of coffee, and there were more beverages and snacks on the counter. Deirdre knew this meant that Joe and Marcy were ready to hear all of the relevant details of Deirdre's latest investigative report. If they were satisfied with the initial report, they'd offer direction, helpful sources, the usual warnings to be careful and call them if she needed help. This meant she had the okay to move ahead full force with the investigation. If they weren't satisfied, they'd ask her to slow it down while they checked on any legal or potential politically sticky issues. The latter only happened once, when Deirdre was new to the *Daily Sun*.

"Right. And there's more." Deirdre straightened the collar of her blouse so that it rested easily on her natural chic style burgundy suit. She addressed Joe, Marcy and Curtis. "Rightway Security doesn't do any other work. Its only contract is with the Prairie Brook housing project. It seems that Rightway Security got the job through a recommendation from someone in the Police Department, city council or even higher up. And from the word on the street, there's another source of drugs – pure, clean drugs – probably from a medical facility in the area. Those drugs are showing up in the same part of town."

"Same drug ring? Different source?" Marcy pushed several strands of her long blonde hair behind her right ear.

"Probably a different source. Could be same drug ring, though." Deirdre looked at the photographer. "Curtis, what do you think?"

"I think it's someone working with the security company. Just a little bonus, ya know. These guards don't make much money. So, if they can cut a deal on the side and line their pockets, well, why not? Seems like everyone's running a scam on the next guy. So, the guard figures if his boss can cut a deal, then why not do the same? Especially if a guard has a source within a pharmacy, hospital or something like that. Then the guard can get access to those pure drugs like Norco, Demerol, Vicodin, Percocet or OxyContin. Now you're talking about bringin' in some real money." He cleared his throat. "My gut says that drug lord Victor Reeks is involved here. He's the king of covert operations. And someone higher up – I don't know who – a politician, a Judge, is protecting him."

"And you can tell all of this from the photographs?" Joe sounded skeptical. He adjusted his glasses.

"Well, er, not exactly," Curtis stammered. He brushed his hands across his denim jeans.

"But we're going to use the photographs to get our soon-to-be informant to tell all." Deirdre moved forward on her chair, opening up her laptop to look at her notes.

"How's that?" Joe asked.

"Well, we know that councilwoman Janice Tyler is in on this. Her voting record shows that she has opposed nearly all private industry and other city council proposals to develop certain pockets of land in her district. A grassroots organization is now interested in purchasing the property on Pine Street. We think Tyler is funding that group. They buy the property cheap, develop the land and *voila*! Everyone is rich. And there's probably something additional in it for Tyler."

"What do you have that proves *all* or *any* of *that*?" Joe took a gulp of black coffee.

"The photographs only show this." Deirdre pointed to an 8" x 10" glossy, black and white photograph. "At 1 a.m. on Monday, Tyler's assistant is exchanging money for several bags. Some contain pills, some contain what looks like marijuana, and others with a white, powdery substance. She's exchanging the bags for money from well-known drug dealer Victor Reeks. Then, we followed Tyler's assistant, who got in the passenger side of that car and rode a few blocks away. She then got into the passenger side of another car. We traced the plates on both cars, and bingo! The second car is registered in Tyler's name."

"Did you see or get photographs of the drivers?" Marcy leaned forward, pushing her coffee mug aside. Her hair fell loosely towards her face.

"We didn't get a good look or photographs of either of them. They're fuzzy." Deirdre leaned on the chair's armrest.

"Tyler's car doesn't necessarily mean that Tyler's in on this." Marcy shifted in her chair, stretching her long, slender legs. "Really. There's nothing concrete there, and talking to anyone, trying to implicate her puts our relationship with her and her office at risk."

Joe leaned forward, releasing the strain on his shirt buttons. He set his mug on the table and sat at the edge of his chair. "Marcy has a good point there." He picked up his pen and began tapping it on the table. "It is interesting that Tyler's been pushing for that minimum security federal prison in her district though." He put the pen down and leaned back in his chair. The middle button of his shirt was strained. "The residents there don't seem happy about it, so I'm not sure why she'd risk alienating her otherwise loyal constituents. Can you dig deeper into that Deirdre?" Joe blinked and raised his gaze to meet Deirdre's face.

Deirdre ran her fingers through her hair. "Sure." She cleared her throat. "I know we still have work to do. Rest assured though, we have photographs *and video* of this exchange. We're going to put the pressure on our street sources, maybe even Reeks. We just got this information during the wee hours this morning, so I'm still thinking about our next move." Deirdre drummed her fingers on the laptop's cover, relieved to see Joe's buttons recede.

"Reeks won't talk. He has good lawyers. And he knows it." Marcy massaged the back of her neck as if to work out a kink. "And you don't have anything concrete on Tyler here. Her assistant, a car registered with her name. Tyler could deny knowing about any of it."

"Whheeew," Joe whistled and nodded toward Deirdre and Curtis. He smiled. "That's quite some work y'all have done. I'm proud of you both. I know you've heard this before, but I'm going to say it again. Stay safe." He pressed his fingertips together and moved his hands to his mouth, then placed them in front of him, pointing toward Deirdre and Curtis. "I know we're not ready for this story to break yet, but when it does, we'll have another award for excellence in reporting."

"And probably a few lawsuits," Marcy smirked.

"Well, I have to give Curtis the kudos here," Deirdre motioned towards him. "He has this undercover photography/videography down to a science. Exactly where we should hide and set up to get the best angles. He's a real photo genius," Deirdre praised.

"Teamwork." Curtis blushed.

Joe placed his hands firmly on the table and cleared his throat. "I *know* this is a big story, so let's keep working it. In the meantime, it seems Morgan has something just as big in the works." Joe stirred his coffee and tapped the stirrer against the mug. "I was summoned by the big dog upstairs." Joe pointed upwards with his coffee stirrer, placing it beside his coffee mug. The newspaper publisher's office was on the top floor of the building. "SAPD Police Chief called this morning, asked us to work with them on what appears to be a homicide."

"My neighbor!" Deirdre stood up and began pacing. "Jimmy Lee Hayden – the busy body on the block – was found dead at 2 a.m."

"For the record," Joe interrupted, "Detective Stuart Beaumont wants to get an official statement from you on your whereabouts last night." Joe looked from Deirdre to Marcy. "He said he talked to you this morning, and y'all discussed something about an exclusive."

Marcy cleared her throat. "You've talked to him already?"

There was a knock on the door. Joe's assistant entered and handed him a note. "Thanks," he nodded and smiled. "Hate to cut this tea party short, but looks like Detective Beaumont is here for that statement now."

* * *

Stuart hadn't been to a newsroom in more than a decade. The frequent buzzing of telephones, constant tap-ta-tap-ta-tap of the keyboards, humming of the newswire machines, and busy atmosphere reminded him of the days when he and his father worked together. It was ironic that it was the news room – more specifically the press room – that relentlessly and mercifully took his father from him.

The managing editor's assistant personally escorted Stuart and Mike Roberts to the conference room. Stuart scanned the walls, which were decorated with framed clippings of some of Deirdre's front-page news reports. Also on display was her Associated Press award for "Truth in Journalism."

Truth – his father's whisper treaded lightly through his head. Stuart tried to push away the accompanying vision.

"Thank you." Stuart nodded to Joe's assistant. "We can find our way from here." Stuart and Mike entered the conference room. Mike carried a briefcase.

Stuart saw a thin, well-dressed, blonde-haired woman and a short, slightly overweight man standing in front of a round conference table. Deirdre sat at the table. Next to her was an early-20s-looking man who wore a polo shirt and blue jeans.

The woman extended her hand to Stuart. "I'm Marcy Cavarino, lead attorney with the *Daily Sun*."

"And I'm Joe Brown, managing editor." Joe's friendly smile met with a firm handshake. He motioned for Stuart and Mike to sit at the table.

"Homicide Detective Stuart Beaumont and Detective Mike Roberts," Stuart said as they eased into the chocolate brown leather chairs. "I appreciate you making time for us. I know the news room can be a busy place, especially with mornings like these." Stuart looked toward Deirdre.

Marcy glanced at her watch.

"And likewise with police stations," Joe added.

"Right." Stuart acknowledged. "So, let's get right to it. After the Chief spoke with your publisher, we decided to forego any formal statement regarding Miss Morgan's whereabouts last night."

Marcy sat back in her chair, relaxed.

"But we would like to spend an hour or so with Miss Morgan right now to gain some insight about the neighborhood and gather information that may prove crucial as our investigation continues." Stuart turned to Marcy and Joe. "If you'd like to stay while we document Miss Morgan's observations, that's fine."

"Thank you. I will stay." Marcy didn't hesitate.

"Curtis and I have a lot of ground to cover, so we'll leave y'all alone." Joe and Curtis stood. "There's plenty of soda, coffee and snacks on the counter." Joe pointed towards the counter at the far wall. He and Curtis walked out and closed the door behind them.

"A soda break sounds good." Deirdre closed her laptop and gathered her pen and pocket calendar as she stood.

As Deirdre walked across the room, Stuart noticed her shapely legs. *Tae Kwon Do workouts.*

When Deirdre returned to the table, she plunked down her pocket calendar and pen, then sat down in the chair next to Stuart's. She scooted the chair slightly forward so there was little distance between them. Deirdre crossed her legs, sat up straight and looked him straight in the eyes.

Fearless.

"Let's get right down to business, because I have an extremely busy schedule ahead of me."

Stuart liked her direct approach.

"Jimmy Lee Hayden wasted enough of my time when he was alive. I don't expect his death to take up major chunks of my time, too."

"Also." Deirdre leaned forward, grasped for her pen, which sent her pocket calendar straight to the floor. It flung open to Friday's date. Stuart noticed many handwritten notes crammed into corners, several items scratched out and asterisks dotted the landscape of her daily activities. There was not a quarter inch of empty space. He also noticed a pink highlighted appointment, "Bible Study" with a scratch mark halfway through it.

Stuart reached to retrieve the appointment book, when he felt the softness of Deirdre's hand brush against his as she snatched the book closed. She placed it squarely on the table.

Her eyes met his. "I will answer any questions that you have, but I'd appreciate it if in the future you make an appointment with me and not go through the *Daily Sun's* executives." Stuart noticed how the determination in her emerald-green eyes was complemented by the deep burgundy tone of her suit.

"Fair enough." Stuart sat back in his chair, meeting Deirdre's gaze.

Detective Mike Roberts slid two manila file folders out of his briefcase. He stood and walked over to Stuart, handing him the two folders. One was marked "Evidence" and the other "Reports." Detective Roberts returned to his seat, opened his notebook, and placed a tape recorder on the table.

Stuart nodded to Detective Roberts, who then spoke into the recorder: "Monday, June 15, 3 p.m. *Daily Sun* office. Informal statement – Deirdre Morgan interviewed by Detective Beaumont."

Stuart turned to Deirdre. "Ready to begin?"

"Yes."

"Miss Morgan, can you please give us your name, date of birth and current address?"

"Deirdre Morgan. August twenty-sixth. 12 Kensington Circle. San Antonio, Texas."

"And you do understand that this interview is being recorded."

"Yes. I do."

"Okay." Stuart didn't like what he was about to do, but it was necessary to the case. He placed the manila folder marked "Evidence" on the table. "Miss Morgan, if you agree, I am going to share with you a photo from the homicide scene of Jimmy Lee Hayden. This photo has been marked up and sections blocked out by SAPD investigators, so as to be less graphic, but since you are familiar with the victim and the location – even the inside of the residence, we hoped that you could provide us some insight. Is that okay with you?"

"Yes, that's fine." She reached down for her soda can.

"Tell me, Miss Morgan. What do you see in this photo?" Stuart placed the photo in front of Deirdre, watching for any non-verbal clues. He immediately noticed Deirdre's fingers tightly clench around her soda can. With the other hand she slowly reached for her necklace.

CHAPTER FOUR

Jimmy Lee Hayden's eyes, empty and eerie stared at Deirdre from the stark backdrop of the marked-up glossy, black-and-white photo. His body was on its back. His head was turned to the side. Blood had trickled down the front and side of his neck and covered the upper part of his chest. *Into Your Hands. Thy soul doth keep. Some laid to forever rest. Others will weep.*

Deirdre remembered the rhyme from her 3rd grade Sunday school class. It was based on the Book of Daniel, Chapter 12, Verse 2. Although Sunday School was decades ago, the rhyme seemed very relevant today and so was the verse:

> *And many of those whose bodies lie dead and buried will rise up, some to everlasting life and some to shame and everlasting contempt. Daniel 12:2 (The Living Bible)*

Deirdre strained to decipher what was sticking out from Jimmy Lee Hayden's neck. It appeared to be about five inches long by one inch wide and was square on the end. The SAPD's notations on the photo made it difficult for Deirdre to view all of the details. But there was one disturbing item that Deirdre strained to place into focus. If her suspicions proved true, the necklace that appeared nearly off the frame of the photo – on the floor located about a foot in front of Jimmy Lee's body was one that Grand Master Kim handed out to all First Degree Black Belts.

Deirdre reached for her necklace. Then she remembered that she lent it to her neighbor, Letty.

"Ahem," Stuart's closeness enveloped her like a sweaty T-shirt after a long, grueling workout. "What do you see?" Stuart asked.

One hand still clenched around the soda can, Deirdre slowly loosened her grip on it, thankful for its cold reminder of the task in front of her. *Stay cool. Stay calm.*

"I see Jimmy Lee Hayden dead, and therefore resigned to the fact that his trouble-making days are over."

Stuart leaned forward, placing his hands on the table, as if to frame the photo. "Okay. Fair enough. Anything else?"

"That's about it."

"Thanks." Stuart continued as he placed the photo back into the folder. "Miss Morgan, what was your impression of Jimmy Lee Hayden when he was alive?"

"Jimmy Lee Hayden was a bully. Plus, he was a free-loading, unintelligent, misinformed bigot. He lived off of his wife and had nothing better to do all day but be the self-appointed neighborhood watchdog." Deirdre took a breath. "His ignorance surfaced when he tried – as he often did – to take the law into his own hands. He violated other people's personal space, individual rights as homeowners and responsible, self-supporting citizens." She paused. "And those were his good traits." Deirdre sat back in her chair, feeling relieved.

Marcy tensed up. She sat on the edge of her chair, arms crossed in front of her.

"Those are strong words," Stuart said. "Could you describe some of the incidents to me, in chronological order, if possible?"

Deirdre took a moment to reflect, but her thoughts were not on her dead neighbor, Jimmy Lee Hayden, but on the man seated next to her. Deirdre had watched Stuart's movements closely – how he commanded a presence as he walked across the room – just as a lion's confident yet graceful strides through a jungle command a regal audience. His deep voice, strong hands and deep brown eyes dominated the room.

A long, cool drink was in order, but Deirdre took a quick sip of her soda instead. "When I picked out the lot for my home – it was a site where a previous older home had been knocked down. So, it was sandwiched between two houses that had also been there for years. As new construction on my home started, my friend – a civil engineer – and I would visit frequently. Jimmy Lee would come over and talk to my friend about how noisy the construction was, and how the noisy equipment woke him up. As my house began to take shape, Jimmy Lee became bolder in his comments about everything. It was apparent that he was walking through my house often, and I got the idea that he was annoyed that a new neighbor was in town. On a few visits, he dropped bigoted remarks and racial slurs. He referred to Mexican-American workers in very negative terms. He made awful racial remarks. Basically, he had a derogatory term for every nationality. Deirdre shook her head.

"Finally, my closing date came. After signing the closing contract of my newly built home, I anxiously drove there with my rental van full of home articles and personal items. It was my first home, and I was pretty excited." Deirdre smiled. "When I arrived, I couldn't get into my driveway because Jimmy Lee had parked in front of *my driveway* and had dumped a 10-foot-wide, 10-foot-high pile of dirt on it. He came out of his house and began shoveling the dirt into the drainage ditch between our homes."

"You thought he did this on purpose to upset you?" Stuart asked.

"I don't know why he did it. But he was parked in front of my driveway and filling in a drainage ditch put there for a good reason by engineers. When I asked Jimmy Lee what he was doing, he said, 'Those engineers don't know what they're doing. I'm just gonna fill 'er up with dirt.' I was able to convince him to move his truck and then tried to reason with him and his wife, Charlene, about the drainage ditch, but they were convinced that they knew best. They said they could do what they liked with the drainage ditch because it was part of their neighborhood."

Stuart read from one of the police reports: "Finally, the homeowners association, builder's representative and engineers visited Jimmy Lee on separate occasions and told him he was in violation of a city ordinance, possibly voiding his own as well as your warranty on the homes' foundations."

"Right." Deirdre's mouth was dry. She sipped her soda and moved to the edge of her chair. "So, he had to remove the dirt from the drainage ditch." Deirdre studied Stuart's hands as he wrote notes.

"What was his wife's reaction to all of this?"

"Charlene stayed in the background, prodding him." Deirdre paused. "My impression of her is that she is a stand-by-your man-no-matter-what gal."

"Okay, go on."

Deirdre enjoyed relating these stories to Stuart. He put her at ease. It was like talking to a longtime friend.

"You want the whole year's incidents retold?" she glanced at her watch. "Did you read the police reports?"

"I read them, but your account is much more informative. Please go on." He smiled. "You can give me the condensed version."

"Okay." Deirdre took another sip of her soda and clasped the can. *I need the caffeine. This has been a long day.* "All was quiet for a while. Or, at least if he was doing anything, I didn't notice. Then, this past summer, he started getting bold and crazy. As I stated in the police reports, he called me up swearing because one of my friends was parked in front of his house, and he called the police to ask them to come and remove the car. When they explained they wouldn't do it, Jimmy Lee came over to the house and assaulted my friend." Deirdre pushed away from the table, so she could punctuate her remarks about these events with her arms and hands. She felt her heart beating faster. "We made a police report, but nothing came of it." Deirdre turned and met Stuart's gaze. "Not enough evidence." She shrugged her shoulders. "After that, he came over on Thanksgiving – in the middle of our dinner – and asked that no one park in front of his house." She shook her head. "I didn't even open the door. I just spoke to him through my front window."

"Earlier this Spring, I planted flowers and hedges along my driveway. He called me at 7:30 a.m. – after I'd gone to work. He left a message on my answering machine telling me that I had planted my flowers wrong, and they would die if I didn't plant them correctly. He offered to help me replant them 'the correct way.' I didn't return his call. Later that evening – after I returned from work – Jimmy Lee was landscaping alongside my driveway – on what is my property. He pulled my flowers out and was throwing my flowers, edging and stones on my driveway and at my garage. When I pulled into my driveway and got out of my car, he threw a rock at me, just grazing my head." Deirdre motioned with her hand across her face, displaying where the rock flew.

Stuart interjected. "That's when he was written up and charged with reckless damage, reckless intent and assault?"

"Yes." Deirdre nodded. "But not enough to get a restraining order against him. Because it was just my word," Deirdre gestured towards her chest, "against his." She took a breath and let out a sigh. "What I didn't know was that Jimmy Lee was climbing over my stone fence into my back yard. My neighbor Letty told me that. I started getting the creeps. I had more hedges installed – for privacy and safety. Trespass was added to his charges."

Deirdre admired Stuart's chiseled profile as he read from a report. "That's when Detective Marcus contacted him in writing, advising that 'harassment is a violation of the Texas Penal code, 42.07' and that additional charges may be filed should he not cease all harassment toward you.' Marcus outlined that 'harassment, in any form, is a violation of a person's constitutional right to privacy and is not taken lightly with the District Attorney's office.'" Stuart's eyes met hers, then he continued reading from the report. "And Judge Bigbee gave him only a verbal reprimand."

"Yes, that's typical," Deirdre shook her head in disgust. A cold flash darted through her eyes.

"What was his wife's reaction during these incidents and then after he received the reprimand from Detective Marcus?"

"She denied his aggressive behavior and assaults. She did make a point to tell the officers that her and Jimmy Lee can replant my flowers because the flowers are part of their neighborhood and on or near their property." Deirdre paused. "After the letter, I didn't see her much. When I did, she had a black-and-blue eye, which he said she got from walking into a door."

Stuart leaned back and made a whistling sound. "Okay, let's jump ahead. When was the last time you saw Jimmy Lee Hayden alive?"

Deirdre sat back to think a moment. "Sunday, late afternoon, about 3 p.m. I was standing in my kitchen talking to one of my friends on the telephone, when I looked out my kitchen window. Jimmy Lee was watering his back lawn and staring at me through the hedges, where there's a break in the stone fence. I didn't realize that my kitchen window was open, and I said to my friend 'You should see what my neighbor is doing now,' and Jimmy Lee immediately stopped staring and retreated inside his house.

"Did Jimmy Lee Hayden ever make a pass at you? Ask you out?"

Deirdre could smell the spicy-sweet scent of Stuart's cologne. She noticed one particular curl in his wavy black hair that fell just below his forehead. She also noticed the distinct dimple in his chin. "Once – he invited me over to play pool with him."

"And what was your response?"

"I told him politely, No. I don't play pool."

"When was that incident on this timeline?"

"That was right after I moved in, in April. I didn't think of it as a pass. I thought he was just being neighborly."

"Hmmm." Stuart closed the file and looked to Detective Roberts. "Anything you want to add?"

"Nope. You got it all." Detective Roberts turned off the tape recorder and then clicked it back on. "End. Monday. June 15. 3:35 p.m. *Daily Sun* office. Informal Statement – Deirdre Morgan interviewed by Detective Beaumont."

"Thank you very much for your time." Stuart extended a handshake to Deirdre. *Strong hands.*

He stood and walked towards Marcy. He reached into his shirt pocket and extended his business card and a handshake to Marcy. "Thank you."

"Off the record," Stuart said, turning to Deirdre. "When will we learn about your whereabouts last night?"

"When you read it in the newspaper." Deirdre stood and straightened her skirt. She tossed her soda can into the trash.

"Hey, nice shot." Detective Roberts piped in. Deirdre turned towards Detective Roberts and smiled.

"*When* do you think it will be in print?" Stuart asked.

"We really can't address that." Marcy stood. "Ms. Morgan's work is highly sensitive, far-reaching and not really predictable. Her keen investigative reporting skills don't just keep these walls well decorated." Marcy looked around at the framed headlines and awards. "Deirdre's work keeps our streets safe, too. The *Daily Sun* reports the news – as quickly and accurately as humanly possible. Reporting the news is a lot like investigating a crime – completely spontaneous. When something comes up, you're on the scene, investigating. And if we're any good, we have someone there observing, reporting. Our lines of work really are not that different."

"True." Stuart nodded in agreement. "It's not predictable. And often fast paced."

"Speaking of which," Deirdre interrupted. "When do you think we'll have more information about this case?"

"Soon enough," Stuart responded. "We'll definitely keep in touch."

Deirdre needed to keep up her guard. She suspected that Stuart was involved with corrupt officials, whose tactics were underhanded and often fatal.

Deirdre knew that she had to talk to Letty about that necklace. Had Letty returned it to her? Not only was Deirdre's life on the line, but after what she saw today, Stuart could place her at the murder scene and possibly find a way to frame her for Jimmy Lee Hayden's murder.

* * *

As Stuart and Mike made their way out of the newsroom, Stuart reflected on Deirdre's responses. He envisioned Deirdre boldly confronting her neighbor who, from the reports that he read, must have stood at least a foot over her petite frame. Yet Deirdre had the self-confidence of a tigress.

Once outside, Mike turned to Stuart. "Wow! She's not afraid of much. Do you think this Hayden guy had the hots for her?"

"Yeah, but she seems oblivious to that fact. I'll say this. Hearing her relate the events is much more interesting and informative than our reports." Stuart reflected for a moment, thinking about Deirdre's movements. How she became more animated when she talked about Jimmy Lee Hayden's odd behavior. He liked the way she moved. He also remembered how soft her hand felt against his. "I find her straightforwardness refreshing, and I can see why the Chief wants to use her to gain insight into this case. I just don't think it's safe. Plus, she did try to make the department look bad in the Alarcon case."

"I might agree with you about it being dangerous, but I think she did lay off in that *other* matter," Mike said.

"Let's meet with him later today or first thing in the morning. See if we can convince him to leave her out of this."

Stuart spent enough time around the news room with his father to know that journalists sometimes ran with what little information they had so that they could be the first to break the news. Sometimes when they did that, they lost their chances for a bigger story. He had witnessed it many times growing up. An overanxious reporter's loyalty to the published word – to leak what little information was available – overrode his or her search for the truth. Deirdre Morgan was one and the same. He'd let her overzealous reporter's instincts take over. That would give the Chief cause to lose confidence in her.

Unless she was really that good of an investigative reporter. If she had intelligence and self-discipline, then he'd have to try another approach. He'd test just how fearless she was.

CHAPTER FIVE

The fuchsia and bright red blooms of the oleander plants lined the highways along Deirdre's route home. Today, she was glad to get out of the noisy newsroom and the city. *What a full day*, she thought. Because of the day's events, Deirdre was feeling pulled in many ways and a bit distracted. She took a few moments to reflect. She knew that there was nothing this life could throw at her that wasn't confronted and overcome by Christ's sacrifice. Jimmy Lee's murder bothered her, and seeing her necklace at the homicide scene frightened her. But she had to remind herself that she is a child of God and that He is always watching out for her. Deirdre felt herself relax as she thanked God for her blessings. That always helped her keep a perspective on earthly things.

Dear Lord, thank You for the weather, my health, my job, my relationship with you, my family and my friends, and please give me strength and wisdom to continue my work. Please give me the discernment to know who to trust, and please protect Curtis, Marcy and Letty. Please also, Lord, be with Charlene Hayden and her family and all those who are suffering because of their loss. Please be with me, Lord, as I visit with them today. You know my fears and my anxiety. Please strengthen my faith in You so that I can confront and overcome those fears.

Deirdre tuned her radio to KDRY Christian Radio, welcoming some good news. KDRY's call letters were derived from its owner Samuel Moss, who was a big believer in keeping Texas as a dry state. How things change, Deirdre thought, as she drove by San Antonio's Pearl Brewery, located on U.S. Highway 281, just north of downtown San Antonio.

Deirdre made a mental list of the ingredients for the seven layer dip that she would prepare for her and Letty's visit to her now-widowed neighbor Charlene Hayden. As she approached her home, Deirdre noticed a group of neighbors and friends who were standing on Charlene's front porch. As Deirdre pulled in to her own driveway, the friends and neighbors turned to look at her. Deirdre smiled and waved. She made eye contact with one man, who just shrugged his shoulders and then turned back towards the group. The others didn't acknowledge her greeting.

That may be an indication of how this visit will go, Deirdre thought. *But it's the right thing to do. Besides, I have nothing to hide from these people.*

At 6:45 p.m., Letty arrived at Deirdre's house.

"Hey."

"Hey. How was the rest of your day?" Letty looked anxious to share. She had already called Deirdre a few times to learn about how her witness statement went regarding her dog's passing, but they hadn't discussed much about the murder next door. Deirdre suspected that Letty wanted to do that in person.

"Well, the police have questioned mostly all of the neighbors, and have instructed us not to talk to each other about 'the incident.'" She made quote marks in the air with her fingers. Letty's shoulder-length brown curls bobbed as she pulled out a kitchen chair.

"What's that about?" Deirdre asked.

"Well, the officer told me that directly after an incident," Letty made the quote marks in the air again, "people remember little details and all, but then if they start talking to each other, they start changing their stories based on what other eyewitnesses say they saw. So, they end up with one version of what people saw, and tend to lose the details that may be significant." Letty's blue eyes glanced across the table and then scanned the room.

"Oh, I guess that makes sense." Deirdre paused. "Did the police have any other information for us, the neighbors?"

"Not really. Just that they'd like us to keep an eye out for any strange activity in the neighborhood. Of course, Lucy is all over that. She's organizing an around-the-clock watch schedule."

"Do you think I'll be included on that schedule?" Deirdre smiled.

"Probably not. You know how the neighbors are, always looking for reasons to exclude you. They say, 'She's so busy. We don't want to bother her.' You know how it goes."

"Yes. And I just might be the *strange activity* that they're watching out for." Deirdre smiled.

"In *their* minds, yes. They just don't get a working, single woman. That concept is so foreign to them. Plus, you're from the Midwest, so that adds to their standoffishness." Letty shook her head as if in disagreement. "If I hadn't lived here with my parents before they passed away, I guess I'd be in your same shoes. But I lucked out and am considered part of the neighborhood."

"Yes. San Antonio is interesting that way. When I first moved here, I found it almost intrusive – the way the neighbors were so anxious to meet and greet. I remember, when I first went shopping and used my credit card, and the clerk had glanced at my card, and then thanked me by my name. I thought, 'Oh, great, she probably memorized my card number and expiration date so that she could run up bills on my credit card.' But I've learned over the years that people here are friendly and really want to get to know you. Plus, tradition runs very strong in San Antonio. I actually like that about this town. But to your point, I get the feeling that the neighbors don't really embrace successful, single Midwestern women just yet."

"In time," Letty nodded. "You'd be surprised at how many people on the block do stand up for you. "There are even a few who would like to get close enough to 'embrace' you." Letty giggled.

"Dave?"

"Yes, he always asks about you. Do you think you'd ever go out with him? He's really a nice guy and gets along with all of the kids in the neighborhood. He may be at Charlene's when we go over."

"Speaking of Charlene's, what's our agenda here? Do we need to stay long, or can we make it a brief 'hello, sorry about your loss,' stay long enough to be polite and hightail it out of there?"

"Well, from what Lucy says, that might be best." Letty hesitated. "You know that Lucy is trying to point the finger at you or at least raise suspicions of your whereabouts that night." Letty shook her head, her curls following her graceful movements. "I think it's ridiculous. That woman doesn't know what she's sayin'. I declare, she talks incessantly and never stops to think or barely to take a breath ... ever. It really wears on me." Letty paused. "However, there's one caveat about our visit next door."

"What?" Deirdre gently sprinkled chopped green onions over the top of the seven-layer dip, which she prepared in a glass casserole dish.

"If Dave is there, we stay for a bit," Letty smiled. She had a cute smile, thanks to her orthodontist.

"I don't think so," Deirdre laughed as she rolled her eyes. Deirdre covered the casserole dish containing the dip with plastic wrap. "We've got to think about Charlene and how she feels." Deirdre picked up the dish, and took a deep breath. "Okay," she let out her breath. "Let's go."

Letty stood. She carried a bouquet of flowers. The ladies walked almost ceremoniously next door.

Arriving at the front door, Letty lightly knocked while Deirdre took another deep breath to calm herself. Lucy answered. Deirdre noticed the look on Lucy's face as a mixture of horror, surprise and shock. Deirdre made a mental note to get Letty's take on that later.

Lucy was about 5 feet 2 inches tall, and weighed nearly 200 pounds. Her dark hair hung loosely around her full round face while a few strands stuck to her protruding cheeks. When she began to speak, the deep wrinkle lines around her mouth and eyes were accentuated.

"This is for Charlene," Deirdre held out the seven layer dip as if presenting a peace offering. Lucy paused. Deirdre pushed the casserole dish forward so it was just inches from Lucy's full, rotund chest.

"Oh," Lucy hesitated. "How nice of you to come." She forced the words, as she turned slightly, motioning for them to come inside.

"How is Charlene?" Deirdre asked.

"As well as can be expected. She's taking medicine to keep her calm. I think she's still in shock. *Pobrecita.*" Lucy took the casserole dish.

One of the endearing qualities of San Antonio culture is the mixture of Spanish and English vocabulary, otherwise referred to as "Spanglish." "*Pobrecita,*" meaning "poor girl," was one of those words that was used and understood by English and Spanish speakers alike.

"Have the police told her anything yet?" Letty piped in. Deirdre was impressed with Letty's curiosity and straightforward approach.

"No, nothing. Her husband is dead. That's all they know." Lucy's footsteps were heavy as she walked in front of them, leading them past the front living – *a.k.a.* "murder" – room and into the more casual, and now crowded, family room.

Deirdre observed a noticeable silence when she, Lucy and Letty approached the entrance of the family room. Deirdre heard Dave's voice from near the back of the room.

"Here's our resident news reporter, we can ask her now." Dave stepped forward from a small group of people who were in a discussion in the far corner of the room. Deirdre noticed how Dave's shirt stretched across his muscular, broad chest.

Deirdre's eyes met Dave's. He winked. "Miss Morgan, maybe you can settle a small disagreement we're having about print versus electronic media."

"I can try," Deirdre responded, grateful for the distraction.

Dave cleared his throat. "Tom here insists that print reporters have some influence over the electronic media portion of the newspaper. Joe and a small group, me included, say that the electronic media is totally independent in its reporting except that it gets its leads and sometimes prints news articles in their entirety from the print news. Jerry and I and company believe that electronic media is neither limited by nor dependent upon the print media."

"You are correct," Deirdre smiled. *Impressive. He is sort of cute when he's right. But he doesn't have the depth in his eyes that Stuart Beaumont has. Stop!* Deirdre reprimanded herself. *Do not think about Stuart right now.*

Standing in the Hayden's home, Deirdre couldn't help but recall the photo that Stuart Beaumont had shared with her earlier that day. *The gold charm necklace.* Deirdre remembered. *I must ask Letty if she still has that necklace.*

Charlene entered the room, fumbling with tattered tissue. Her tear-stained face, coupled with red, bloodshot eyes was a sign of how she was coping with her loss.

"I think he'll be home soon," she cried as she spoke to no one in particular and stared down at her tissue. "I just think he'll come through the door as if he's returning from the grocery store," she looked up and scanned the crowded room of people. "I just can't believe he's gone." When Charlene saw Deirdre, Charlene stopped and slumped, steadying herself by leaning her shoulder against the wall.

Lucy nearly knocked over a plate of food as she rushed to Charlene's side, grabbing Charlene's arm and guiding her away from the family room.

"Is that? Is that who I think it is?" Charlene's voice trailed off as Lucy led Charlene into the kitchen.

"Let's get you some water," Lucy said to Charlene. "You need to drink water. It's good for you. You have cried a river and then some already. You need water or you'll get dehydrated."

Deirdre looked for Letty, who was talking with Dave and his friends in the far corner of the room. Deidre wanted to leave, but didn't want to seem too obvious. She walked over to Letty as nonchalantly as possible.

"Deirdre, don't take that to heart," said Letty. "Charlene is not in a normal state right now. She is grieving, and I'm sure she hasn't slept much."

"Who could?" Dave piped in. "I wake up about every hour since this happened. Any little sound and I'm out of bed, checking that my doors are locked and my windows secured. Who knows if someone is targeting this neighborhood or if this was just a random act of violence? We just can't be too cautious, and I'm definitely in the alert mode now."

"It's good to be keenly aware of our surroundings," Deirdre agreed. "But I wouldn't lose any sleep over it."

"Sure," Letty interjected. "That's easy for you to say. You have a black belt in karate."

"Tae Kwon Do," Deirdre said quietly, wishing she had never mentioned her martial arts training to Letty. "Oh, by the way, Letty, remember that necklace you borrowed ... the one with the Tae Kwon Do charm?"

"Yes."

"Did you ever return it to me? I'm going to see Grand Master Kim and I'd like to –"

"Whoa, whoa!" Dave interrupted. "Grand Master? Black Belt? Letty, did you say that Deirdre has a black belt in karate?" Dave looked at Deirdre up and down. His eyes sparkled as he smiled.

"Yes, so she can defend herself," Letty said.

"I probably know just enough to get myself hurt," Deirdre said modestly. She lowered her voice to just above a whisper, hoping that Letty and Dave would follow suit and keep their voices down.

"Letty," Deirdre continued. "I think I'm going to head out."

"I don't think you should go just yet," said Letty. "You have no reason to run out of here."

"I'm not running, and I think Charlene's feelings are what are most important now. She's upset, and seeing me didn't make her feel any better. I've paid my respects. I hope she knows I'm here for her if she needs me."

"We'll walk you home, Deirdre," Dave grabbed Letty's arm and headed towards the front door. Before Deirdre or Letty could protest, all three of them had left the Hayden's home, and were standing in front of Deirdre's house.

Suddenly, Deirdre heard car tires squealing, as a black Cadillac dashed around the corner, heading straight toward the Haydens' home.

"What's going on here?" Dave said aloud, as he grabbed both of them, practically dragging them behind the stone fence of Deirdre's house.

The three of them peered out from behind the fence as the Cadillac sped down the street, did a three-point turn in the middle of the street, and slowly drove up the street, pausing when it was in front of the Haydens' driveway.

Deirdre strained to see if she could view the car's license plates. A woman wearing a baseball cap slowly got out of the passenger side of the car, then crouched down and ran towards the front of Charlene Hayden's home. The woman, whose hair was stuffed in the cap, stooped between bushes in front of the house, placed her face nearly against the glass as she peered into the home's front window. After about 30 seconds, the woman turned and scurried back to the car. When she opened the passenger car door, the overhead light came on, and Deirdre caught a glimpse of the driver's face. Something stirred her memory, but she couldn't quite place it. The woman began speaking to the driver when he suddenly slapped her across the top of the head as he motioned for her to close the door. The overhead light extinguished. After a short pause, the car sped back down the street.

The front door of the Hayden home opened.

Letty, Dave and Deirdre ducked farther behind the fence.

"Did I hear something?" Lucy's voice sounded familiar.

"Probably just a bunch of kids." Charlene Hayden's voice was distinctive, and it sounded like the two of them had walked out, onto the front porch.

A cell phone rang. "Hello," Charlene answered. "Uh-huh."

Deirdre heard the voices and footsteps retreat, and the front door closed behind Charlene and Lucy.

"Hey." Deirdre had Dave and Letty's attention. Deirdre motioned for them to go to her back door.

"What was that about?" Dave looked to Deirdre and Letty for answers.

"She's the investigative reporter." Letty turned to Deirdre.

"Did anyone get the license plate number?" Deirdre asked as she jotted notes into a pad of paper. "Oh, and while I'm thinking of it, Letty, will you please check to see if you still have my gold Tae Kwon Do necklace?"

"Okay, but what do you think that was about?" Deirdre sensed that Letty wasn't going to change the subject. "A man and a woman at the Hayden home? This late at night? And in such a hurry?"

"They weren't exactly *at* the Hayden home," Deirdre pointed out. "They went *to* the Hayden home, went *near* the Hayden home, but didn't actually go *into* it."

"Maybe they had the wrong address," Dave suggested.

"Or maybe they were casing the house," Letty said. "Through my volunteer work at the hospital, I have learned that there are people who read obituaries and then rob the home while the family is at the wake, rosary or funeral."

"That's sad, but true," Deirdre added.

"Or maybe the person who killed Jimmy Lee Hayden was coming back to the scene of the crime." Letty made quotation marks in the air again. "Maybe they forgot something in the house. A piece of evidence." Letty's voice escalated as the words raced from her mouth.

"Wow, Letty, you are all about this crime mystery business, aren't you?" Dave interjected.

"Really." Deirdre agreed.

"I read a lot of mystery novels," Letty blushed. "And Deirdre's news reports," she added.

Deirdre looked at her watch. "Well, friends, I'd love to stay up and solve this mystery, but it's been a long day, and I believe that tomorrow will be just as hectic. I'm going to call it a night."

"Hey, Letty, I've got a pot of coffee ready to brew, if you want to come over for a bit before turning in," Dave offered.

I might just do that," Letty said, as the two of them started to walk away.

* * *

Stuart and Mike waited in the Police Chief's office in silence. It was comforting, Stuart thought. In the way that quiet is welcome only in the presence of a close friend or family member.

The coveted first appointment on the Chief's schedule was theirs. Barring any emergencies, the Chief would meet them directly after his 6:45 a.m. meeting in the briefing room.

Stuart heard footsteps outside the door. He began to stand. Mike followed. "Good Morning, Chief," Stuart greeted him. "Hope you don't mind us hanging out here this morning."

"No problem." The Chief motioned for them to sit down. "So, what's up?" The Chief tossed his cell phone on his desk as he plunked down in his highback, black leather chair. "And has that reporter, Morgan, been any help to y'all?" The Chief's chiseled profile, clean-shaven face and neatly pressed uniform made Stuart feel as if he was talking to a corporate CEO.

"Well, that's what we wanted to talk about, Chief." Stuart was determined. "Mike and I interviewed her yesterday, took a statement, and showed her some of the crime scene photos. And we both agree that we'd like to keep Deidre Morgan far away from this case."

The Chief shifted in his chair.

Stuart continued. "There seems to be some interesting twists in this case. We found the murder weapon. The lab is searching for identifiable prints. We found a prescription form, some narcotics – they may check out as legal prescription drugs. We have a neighbor, who has made a statement that she saw Morgan or someone coming to or from Morgan's house that night, and evidence at the crime scene that may link Morgan to the murder."

The Chief waved his hand as if to dismiss that idea. "That's ridiculous. Morgan as a suspect." He brought his hand to his chin. "The *Daily Sun's* publisher vouches for Morgan's whereabouts that evening. But it is an interesting lead that needs to be followed," the Chief continued.

Stuart shifted his weight. "My first priority, Chief, is everyone's safety." Stuart continued. "I think there's too much friction in the neighborhood for Morgan to be any use to us. Plus, I think it may be dangerous for her to feed information to us when the neighbors seem suspicious of her activities anyway. She *is being watched*," Stuart emphasized the last part of his statement.

"Well, that's a pretty easy fix." The Chief looked at Stuart. "You know how we keep Morgan safe, right?" He met Stuart's gaze.

"Are you suggesting ...?" Stuart hesitated.

"Yes. Let's do it by this afternoon." The Chief stood. "Keep me apprised of your progress."

Mike nodded and stood.

"Yes, sir." Stuart stood.

Together, Mike and Stuart walked out of the Chief's office.

Just outside the door, Stuart froze. He stood in the hallway with his hands clasped together, his gaze fixed on the floor.

"Stuart, you okay?" Mike turned to Stuart, waiting.

Stuart felt his jaw tighten.

"So, you don't think much of the Chief's plan."

"He gave us an order." Stuart's teeth ground together.

"I'll get a patrol car and an officer, L.G. Okay?"

Stuart nodded. "I'll be in my office. Call when they're ready." Stuart rubbed his jawbone as he made his way to his office. He didn't realize he was clenching his jaw so hard.

Once at his office, Stuart locked the door behind him. He went to his desk, pulled open the top drawer. Stuart knew he must remain calm. Bold action was needed, not weakness and self-pity, however justified.

He touched the Bible that was settled in his top drawer, pulled it out, closed the drawer and knelt beside his desk. Intertwined his fingers and bowed his head.

"Our Father, who art in heaven ..." Dire circumstances called for prayer by the book.

"... Amen" Stuart heard some commotion in the hallway and then silence, except for his own breathing. "Lord, help. I know you put me in this place at this time, but please forgive my weakness, my doubt." Stuart's bottom lip quivered. "I am not worthy of You. I never will be." Stuart clenched his hands tightly together. "I know that the lashings and scars that Your Son suffered through are for my sins. I know that, and I am sorry. And thank You for the gift of Your Son. Thank You." Stuart was moved by the magnitude of His sacrifice. "I know my suffering seems minor, but I really need You to give me strength now. I need You to help me be a warrior of justice for You, if that is Your plan. I need You to increase my faith." Stuart felt a tear form. "Please, Lord, let me know that I am doing the right thing ... maybe a sign."

Stuart heard the familiar sound of his cell phone. He reached into his pocket. "Beaumont."

"The patrolman's out front." Mike spoke clearly. "It's officer Morgan – John Morgan."

"No relation, is it?"

Stuart heard Mike exhale. "No, I checked." Mike chuckled. "I thought the same thing ... Odd right?"

"Yeah." Stuart closed his eyes. He felt the rough leather cover of his Bible beneath his fingers. "I'll be right there." Stuart stood and headed to meet the patrolman.

CHAPTER SIX

Deirdre sat at her newsroom desk and quickly jotted notes:

"Property – East Side"
"Low security prison facility"
"Hospital – drugs"
"Street – drugs"
"Reeks – tie-in"
"Sonny Mitchell"
"City councilwoman – what profit?"

Deirdre grabbed her notepad and stopped by the break room to refill her morning coffee on her way to the *Daily Sun's* morgue, *a.k.a.* the newspaper's archive room. Tucked in a corner of the newsroom, the 20 x 30 foot morgue had four glass walls. It was adorned with a few wooden chairs and tables covered with newspapers, blank notepads and pens. Laptop computers lined the walls as did old, sturdy wooden index card cabinets filled with microfiche. The morgue reminded Deirdre of her high school library, but an eighth of the size. Deirdre found the news clipping featuring Janice Tyler at an honor event.

City Councilwoman Janice Tyler was San Antonio East Side's longtime representative. Her days dated back to Sonny Mitchell. The article Deirdre found featured East Side citizen Charles Stanton, whose undercover work led to Sonny Mitchell's arrest. Stanton suffered a gunshot wound and was awarded the FBI medal of honor for bravery. He presently served as director of the Scott-Davis YMCA, located on San Antonio's East Side.

Tyler was in the photograph with Stanton at the ceremony. Deirdre browsed the article. The article's last paragraph mentioned a proposal for a low-security federal prison to be housed on the city's East Side. That was nearly five years ago, and Tyler was still pushing for that prison to be located on the East Side. If Deirdre recalled correctly, Tyler had all but one vote needed to gain city council's approval for the plan. Deirdre noted that the proposed facility site and the site currently being considered were different addresses. The current one was close to the apartment complex where the drug activity took place. Why would Tyler want that?

Deirdre went to her computer to search property ownership of the two addresses. The phone rang signaling a call from the receptionist, but Deirdre ignored it. The old adage "follow the money" rang true, and Deirdre wanted to find out who owned these properties.

* * *

"Oh, there she is," the receptionist addressed Stuart Beaumont and a uniformed police officer as she saw Deirdre emerge from the morgue and walk to her desk.

"Thank you. We can find our way from here," Stuart Beaumont said, as he barreled towards Deirdre's desk with the officer close behind.

"But wait. It's ringing ..." the receptionist's call to announce their arrival remained unanswered.

Stuart's heart jumped as he watched Deirdre with her notepad in one hand and reaching for her computer keyboard with the other. Her slender fingers typed swiftly. She was oblivious to Stuart and the officer as they approached her desk. *Looks like she's intent on researching something.* Stuart made a mental note of the website she was browsing, the Bexar County Appraisal District, before he interrupted.

"Deirdre," she turned to face him.

Her eyes widened, and then a line wrinkled between her brows. "What are –?"

Stuart fought his first instinct, which was to reach for her hand, hold it and let her know it would be okay. Instead, he squared his shoulders.

"Deirdre Morgan, you're under arrest." Stuart nearly choked on the words. "You have the right to remain silent..." Stuart continued while the patrolman secured Deirdre's wrists in front of her with a zip tie.

"I don't believe this!" She braced her hip against the desk. "What are you doing? You can't arrest me. I haven't done anything wrong. Plus ... I have to teach a Tae Kwon Do class tonight. They'll be upset if I'm late ... again." She tried to gesture with her restrained hands. "What? Did I allow my inspection sticker to lapse? You guys are getting really touchy these days, aren't you?"

The patrolman led Deirdre away from her desk. Stuart stepped alongside them.

"...anything you say can and will be held against you..." Stuart purposely raised the volume of his voice as they walked by Marcy, the corporate attorney's office.

"What's this about?" Marcy jumped out of her chair and kept up with Stuart, Deirdre and the patrolman's rapid pace as they exited the newsroom.

"Will you represent her?" Stuart looked at Marcy. He wished that he could wink or somehow give her a signal, but his believable performance as the hardnosed detective was critical.

"Of course."

"Bail hearing will be at 3 p.m. at the county courthouse, 2nd floor. See you then." He exited the building.

"This is ridiculous," Deirdre protested louder now that they were outside. She held her head high as if to challenge him. Their eyes met. Something stirred inside of him. She had a spark that was relentless. *Lord, I like her style, but please not now. I need to focus. There's work to do. I can't let a woman complicate things right now.*

Stuart thanked the officer, who nodded at Stuart and then left them alone. Stuart led Deirdre to his unmarked police car, which was parked discreetly along the curb of a quiet street. He opened the passenger's side door. Once inside, Stuart scanned the area for curious onlookers. Confident that they weren't being watched, Stuart reached for Deirdre's wrists.

She pulled away.

Stuart fished a slip-joint knife out of his back pocket and held it up. "I want to release you."

"Oh," she pushed her wrists towards him.

As he sliced and slipped off the zip tie, Stuart noticed the stark contrast of the cold sturdy plastic of the zip ties to Deirdre's warm, soft, delicate skin. He was tempted to pull her wrists towards him, to get closer to her lightly floral scent. He watched as her dusty blonde hair fell softly forward as she looked down at her wrists. *No woman will complicate my life. Not now. Not ever.*

"What are you doing?" Her green eyes softened as she met his gaze.

Stuart noticed her full, moist lips. He turned and placed the keys in the ignition. He stared straight forward to concentrate on the road ahead.

As he drove, Stuart reached for and grabbed an envelope next to him and tossed it to Deirdre. "Recognize this?"

"Sure, it's a brown envelope. I've seen lots of 'em."

"I mean do you recognize what's inside of the envelope?" He hesitated. "Are you always so literal?"

"I *am* a writer."

"Yes. I know."

Deirdre opened the envelope and pulled out a black and white photo. "Yes, I do recognize this. It looks like a photo of one of my kitchen knives."

"Good." Stuart nodded and smiled.

"Good? Good what?" The anger in her voice edged louder. "I'm being arrested because I had a set of old steak knives?" She slammed the photo onto her lap and clenched the edges of the brown envelope. "Excuse me. I didn't realize it was against the law to have old, worn out kitchen utensils." She raised her hands in surrender. "You should have seen the handheld can opener my parents used. I guess I come from a long line of criminals. We should have read the manufacturer's instructions. Is it listed in the fine print?" She slapped her palms against her thighs and the brown envelope fell to her feet.

Stuart enjoyed the sarcasm in Deirdre's voice.

"Okay, I confess." Deirdre flicked her foot and the envelope fell to the floor. "I still do have one old steak knife from that set in my kitchen. But I have tossed the other ones." She stomped on the brown envelope. "Honest. I promise not to use any old kitchen steak knives anymore. And I'll find that old can opener and get rid of it as well. Cross my heart." She made an invisible "x" across her chest.

Stuart's eyes lingered on the imaginary "x" on Deirdre's chest. He quickly raised his eyes to meet hers.

"You have only one of these knives?"

"Yes, I threw away all the rest. The last one I threw away was a coupla' months ago."

Stuart stopped at the traffic light. "Look at that picture closely now. Can you tell if that is one you threw away?" He turned to watch Deirdre as she studied the photograph more intently. He admired her ability to concentrate on the photograph in spite of what seemed to be a dire situation for her.

"Well, yes." She pointed to the photograph. "You can see the worn blade and the mud all over the blade and the handle. I used it to cut the weeds out of my garden. Can't you see the mud?" She turned the photograph towards him as the traffic light turned green.

Green. The color of your eyes. Traffic lights will never be the same. Stuart looked straight ahead as he eased onto the gas pedal. "How about blood?" he noted.

"Blood!" Deirdre tossed the photograph onto the floor and wiped her hands on her skirt as if to wash them. "Eeeeww! You mean to tell me there's blood all over my kitchen knife?"

Stuart felt Deirdre staring at him.

Deirdre's eyes flashed in an instant. "Oh, my goodness. Are you saying that Jimmy..."

"Jimmy Lee Hayden was killed with a steak knife." Stuart finished Deirdre's sentence. "*Your* steak knife," he emphasized. "And I'd bet my badge that you still have one kitchen steak knife in your kitchen drawer. But the investigative team will find that out soon enough."

"So, you're arresting me for murder?" she gasped.

"Well, sort of," he answered. *It is time to be straight with her now.*

"What do you mean, 'sort of'? I want some answers. *Now*." Her voice was crisp and clear. She edged forward in her seat to face him.

Stuart eased the car onto a quiet street and parked. "Deirdre, what I'm about to tell you is to be kept in strict confidence. Do you understand?" He looked deeply into her eyes. The almond-shaped beauties reflected to him that she was no stranger to keeping secrets.

"Of course," she responded.

Stuart moved closer to her. "I had an interesting talk with one of your neighbors, a Mrs. Menendez, yesterday afternoon. She claims that she saw someone come out of the side window of the Hayden home and run into your yard. She identified the knife as one of yours, and she was allegedly the first one who Charlene Hayden called when Charlene found Jimmy Lee's body."

Stuart had just shared information with Deirdre that had not been disclosed to the media: that Charlene Hayden discovered her husband's body and the alleged murder weapon. Disclosing these facts to Deirdre was his way of testing her loyalty to solving the case rather than seeking her own fame. If the information leaked to the media and became headline news, Stuart would have a reason to convince the Chief that the department couldn't rely on Deirdre to be discreet. He didn't mention the necklace.

"Did Lucy say at what time all of this occurred?

"Well, she was a bit cloudy on that issue. She says it was about midnight when she let her dog, Princeton, out. And when she looked out her front window, someone was entering your yard."

"Did she also tell you that she is a narcoleptic?"

"A narco-whatic?"

"Narcoleptic. She doses off. Falls asleep and wakes up hours later unaware that she's been sleeping."

"No. She didn't mention that." Stuart shifted in his seat. "Listen," Stuart changed the subject. "The arrest scene was all a set-up. After talking to Mrs. Menendez and reading the 'Physical Evidence' report, the agents have reason to believe that there's more to this case than meets the eye. Doesn't seem like a random break-in slash murder. Also, it seems that you have more than one nosey neighbor in that neighborhood of yours. And that someone is trying to set you up."

"Why me? I'm just an honest, working girl." She plunked her hands into her lap.

"Yes. That's how it seems to me. You know how it is in your line of work. You step on a lot of toes and anger a lot of people."

"I just publish the truth. If people don't like to read about what they do, they ought to think about it before they do it."

"Do you always live like that?"

"Like what?" She pinned him with a stare.

"Like your life is an open book? Haven't you done things that you may not be proud of, or that you wouldn't want printed in the newspaper?"

"Sure, there are things I wouldn't enjoy reading about myself. Lots of things. But nothing this ... ummm ... lethal. Nothing that I'd go to prison for. Most of my life's stories are adventures."

"Is that how you view it? You delving into the lives of others, publishing their actions, sometimes their deep, dark secrets – it's just an adventure?"

"Yes. I guess that I think of everything in life as an adventure."

"Even this?" They were close to the county jail on South Frio Street, near downtown San Antonio.

Her shoulders sagged. "Yes," she sighed.

"Well, it looks like you're moving forward in your

adventures. You're leaving a whirlwind of activity all around you. It's like the bees are buzzing and some are trying to sting you. But I do admire your determination to just stay full steam ahead. So far, it has kept you from getting stung."

"Right. So far. But it does seem as if I'm a target, and if my neighbors are up to something, they'd use me as the scapegoat because I'm young, single, unpredictable..."

Stuart cut in. "You? Unpredictable? How so?"

"Well, I ... I ... Oh, I don't know. You'll just have to see as you get to know me."

"Oh." He wondered if that was an invitation. He imagined that everything this young beauty did was a well-thought out, well-designed scheme that left no room for unpredictable moves.

"Anyway," Deirdre continued. "Everyone on the block knows that there's no love lost between Jimmy Lee Hayden and me. So, naturally I'd be the one they'd pin it on."

"And you say that you have a concrete alibi?"

"Solid as Jimmy Hoffa's shoes," Deirdre quipped.

"Oh, boy, that's a heavy statement." Stuart couldn't resist the pun, and Deirdre joined him in a short, tension-releasing laugh. He was glad that he could make her laugh. *She is so cute when she smiles. Her entire face lights up.*

Stuart turned to Deirdre in all seriousness.

"Okay, this is business. We've been doing some checking on Jimmy Lee Hayden," Stuart continued. "And he has a real sketchy background. He's never held a decent job. He has a history of some minor incidents, indicating violent behavior. He did go to a court-ordered anger-management class. On top of that, he filed a few civil cases where he sued restaurants, shop owners and even a previous employer for what we call 'slips and falls.' You know, people say they're hurt and sue for damages, workmen's comp, insurance claims."

Deirdre nodded, brows drawn tight over her nose.

Stuart continued. "We can't really account for his daily activities. He made his presence known in the neighborhood, and that may have been a smokescreen. There are a lot of unaccounted-for hours in his days. Something smells fishy. We want to move on this fast."

"Do you think Jimmy Lee led some kind of a double life? He didn't seem very bright. Unless he had everybody fooled."

"Don't get your mind running now." Stuart grinned inside, but spoke with all seriousness. "I wouldn't go that far, but the Chief wants you to observe daily activities in the neighborhood. There's a strong possibility that there's an outside source involved here."

"Oh, I see," Deirdre rubbed her hands together and then held them to her lips. She looked pensive.

"The way he was killed," Stuart brought Deirdre back from her musings. "It seems as if there's a message there; a reason for that kind of killing." Stuart was thinking aloud now. "A steak knife through the Adam's Apple. I wonder if it's gang-related. I mean it seems so Bruce Lee style."

"There is a Lee High School," Deirdre pointed out.

"I'm going to check out any lead I can," Stuart said. "But remember, Deirdre," he said as if he were coaching her. "This is important. You are on our side now. You're not to leak any of this to anyone. Not *anyone*. It's for your own safety. Do you understand?" His voice was almost threatening.

"Look," Deirdre interjected. "Unlike what you may think of newspaper reporters, I can keep a secret." Deirdre pointed her hands toward her chest. "I understand that there's a case to solve here. I am interested in finding and printing the truth, the whole truth and nothing but the truth. But don't talk to me as if I were a child." She held her hands out. "I've worked very hard and very long hours to be good at what I do, and besides, I am a professional print journalist ... and a very good one, I might add. I'm not some bimbo on the nightly news. I have integrity. I do my own research and write my own articles. As a print journalist, I know more secrets than even you'd like to know. You wouldn't believe what people have told me 'off the record.' And that's where it stays: off the record." She cut her hands through the air.

Stuart listened to the underlying roar in her voice. She possessed the gracefulness of a tigress atop a mountain, but threaten her kingdom, her territory ... the news, or more accurately, her search for the truth ... and she was ready to pounce onto her prey ever so delicately, but with fatal effectiveness.

"Are you finished?" Stuart asked. He noticed the ruddiness on her cheeks as she became more animated with her speech.

"Yes," she paused. "For now."

Stuart yanked another zip tie from his pocket. "We're near the county jail, so we have to make this look real. I apologize, but I need to secure this restraint on you."

"Apology accepted. Now, tell me again. What is the purpose of this? And what is the plan?" Deirdre asked as he bound her wrists and she placed them back on her lap.

"The purpose of this set-up arrest is to make the true criminals relax. To make them feel safe so they'll make another move. But this time we'll be watching."

"And I'll be out of jail," she winced, "in let's see" she glanced down at her platinum and gold Timex watch.

Sensible and classy. Stuart was looking at Deirdre's watch, but describing Deirdre. He hated to think that soon all of her valuable items would be placed in a metal box identified only by a case number and her last name, but he knew that this was necessary.

"... it's 12:30 now, so in two and a half hours – at three o'clock, right?" Deirdre looked at Stuart for confirmation.

In her expression, he caught a glimpse of what he imagined was Deirdre Morgan, the little girl. Wide-eyed, yet cautious. Wanting omniscience; willing to forge ahead, but always watchful and observant of ever-present danger.

"That's correct. Three o'clock," Stuart assured her. "Since your bail hearing is in a few hours, and if it's not crowded, they'll keep you in the holding tank, not an actual jail cell."

"Is that good? The holding tank? Isn't that where they take all of the criminals first? I think I'd rather be by myself in a cell."

"Okay, I'll see what I can do." Stuart drove towards the county jail.

* * *

"Thanks." Deirdre hoped she could trust Stuart, especially now when it counted. As they approached South Frio Street, Deirdre saw several news trucks parked in front of the jail. "Well, looks like the media has arrived."

"That's good. We want to get the message out that you've been arrested for Jimmy Lee Hayden's murder."

"I'm ready to go," Deirdre said. "The Channel 4 news truck hasn't arrived yet, so if we go now, Channel 12 will scoop them for the five o'clock news. That would make me happy." She took a breath.

"Okay, then, let's go."

Stuart led Deirdre to the building that housed the jail. As they entered the building, Stuart transferred Deirdre to a police officer. Walking into the lobby, Deirdre's sight was blinded by the flashing lights of photographers' cameras. As the reporters fired questions at her, she gasped for air. She felt as if she were an ant inside of the foundation of a child's sandcastle. With each shovelful of sand, she lost more air, more daylight slipped away. She looked for Stuart in the crowd, but he was nowhere. Deirdre knew she was on her own. And like the tiniest, most determined ant, she climbed to the top of the sandcastle and claimed her reign as queen.

"I'll answer questions after my bail hearing at three o'clock," she answered one reporter. "There is no foundation to these allegations." She fired the answers as quickly as the questions were shot at her. "I will be cleared of all charges, and I will find the real killer of Jimmy Lee Hayden. You can count on that."

CHAPTER SEVEN

"L.G.!" Stuart looked up from his desk as Mike appeared in his office doorway, arms spread and his hands pressed against the door's inner molding.

"What's up?"

"Chief wants to see us. Some urgent business."

Stuart's heart raced as he and Mike walked toward the Chief's office. With his stomach queasy, he felt a dull ache in his head. *Did something happen to Deirdre? I'll never forgive myself if she's hurt.*

Stuart saw the Chief pacing outside his office door. He held a manila folder in one hand as he tapped it against the palm of his other hand.

The Chief looked up and motioned for the men to enter, then closed the door behind them.

"L.G. Mike."

Before the Chief moved away from the door, Stuart asked, "Is it Morgan? Is she okay?"

The Chief turned to look at Stuart. "As fine as someone can be in the county jail. This is on another matter." The Chief continued. "I need y'all to take a quick trip down to Corpus Christi to meet with Detective Maldonado. He has a lead on that drug-trafficking case we've been working, and he has some files that he says we'll need. We couldn't discuss details over the phone, so I said y'all could be there within three hours or less."

Stuart cleared his throat and shuffled in his chair. "What about Morgan? Her hearing is scheduled for three today."

"I'm on top of that," he assured Stuart. "I checked with our guy at the courthouse. Morgan's attorney, Marcy Cavarino, is already there. So, no worries. Plus, Morgan's a tough cookie." He glanced at his watch. "You have reservations at the Best Western on South Padre Island Drive, just over the bridge on the Island. Maldonado's gonna meet you there at 1830."

"Let's get movin'."

Mike's words startled Stuart into action.

* * *

Deirdre heard a door open and footsteps. She eased off of the edge of her cot, trying not to touch anything in the overly bleached smelling 10- by 8-foot cell.

She looked down at the drab gray, concrete floor, searching for some colorful remark as the officer headed closer to her cell. If she could say something witty, it would make her feel more herself and might cheer her up.

Deirdre's county-provided footwear hit the cold floor, the cot springs squeaked, and she walked towards the steel-barred door. Her stomach felt tight. Her hands were shaking.

The officer stopped in front of Deirdre's cell, placed her hand on the handle of her night stick and announced. "Bail hearing is Wednesday morning at nine."

"What!" Deirdre stepped back, wrinkled her brow, waved her arms in front of her, planted them on her hips and stomped her foot on the ground. "Did you say Wednesday morning?"

"Yep." The officer turned to walk away.

"What happened to three o'clock today?"

"Judge got called out on an emergency," the officer walked down the hallway. "All hearings in his courtroom are postponed until Wednesday morning." The *click-click-click* of the officer's footsteps were fading, signaling her retreat. Deirdre didn't want to be alone with nothing to read, no one to talk to. And she still hadn't thought of something sassy.

"Excuse me, officer," the footsteps stopped. "Why do they call those night sticks, anyway?"

"Because when we hit someone over the head, it's 'good night,'" the footsteps continued until all Deirdre could hear was the jingling of keys, followed by the familiar click, turn and release of the lock, the door open and shut. Then silence.

Jailhouse humor. Great. Deirdre turned to look at her cell – which, thanks to Stuart Beaumont, had become home, at least for today and tonight. *Good night. Well, there's an idea.* She wondered what Stuart Beaumont was doing right now.

Why did I trust him? Why would I trust any man? Why am I even here?

Deirdre pulled at her prison attire and held it clenched within her fists. She wanted to scream. Then Deirdre remembered the only One she could trust in: the Good Lord. Deirdre recalled the trials of Paul during his arrests and prison stays in Caesarea and then Rome. She paused, relaxed her hands and folded her arms. *Please, Lord, help me make it through this. Be with me, please. Forgive me for feeling abandoned. I'm sorry. But I do feel very alone and scared.*

She fought back tears of despair as she settled onto the edge of the cot and tried to sleep. Deirdre awoke to sounds of footsteps in the hallway. She used her fingers to gently wipe the teardrops from beneath her bottom lashes before she could focus in on the two figures passing by her cell. Deirdre took a quick, short breath. "It couldn't be."

Deirdre was wide awake now. The hefty female officer was talkative and animated as she led Victor Reeks' girlfriend, the one and only CeeCee McBride, down the hallway toward a nearby cell. As they neared Deirdre's cell, CeeCee's trademark burgundy red hair swung slightly as she turned to nod at Deirdre. The county-issued orange jumpsuit hung on CeeCee's slender frame like an oversized dress on a rag doll. Deirdre recalled the most recent photos of CeeCee with Victor at an art show benefit. CeeCee's clothes were trendy and chic. The orange was not a good look for her.

Deirdre leaned forward on the cot. She strained to observe and hear any of the conversation. The officer led CeeCee to a cell just across the hall and down a few cells from Deirdre's. The officer locked CeeCee's cell without saying a word to her about a bail hearing, then turned, jingled her keys and almost skipped down the hallway. *Jingle, click, turn, release, door open and shut. Then silence.*

"PSSSSST. Hey." Deirdre jumped at the sound, and wasn't surprised that CeeCee breached the rules of silence. Deirdre stood and went to the cell bars.

"Yeah?" Deirdre would break the rules, too. Anything to gain information.

"What are you here for?"

"It's a long story, but mostly murder." Her mind was calculating. How much did she want to reveal?

"What? Did you catch your boyfriend with another chick or somethin'?"

"No. Nothing like that." Deirdre wasn't in the mood to discuss men right now. After Stuart left her in here for this long, she certainly didn't think much of any man right now. "Actually, my neighbor was murdered." Deirdre held onto the bars and tried to see if there was anyone else in the hallway.

"Oh."

"The cops searched all of the neighbors' houses. I had some Coke. I tried to hide it, but it was too late. So here I sit; possession and murder charges." Deirdre didn't consider this a lie; she did have some sodas at home.

"How'd they find it? The coke, I mean?"

"Those sniffing police dogs."

"Oh, yeah, they're real good at what they do."

"Yes. And you? What are you in for?"

"Drug bust. No police dogs though. Just some hearsay and phony eyewitnesses. They got nothin' on me. I'm too good for that."

"Oh." Deirdre paused. "Did you drop the good stuff?" Deirdre used the street lingo that she'd heard so often in her investigative reporting work.

"Oh, yeah. I've got a line on some good stuff." Her voice became more animated. "I mean hospital-grade, prescription only. Ya know, I'm talkin' about Vic, Perc, Ox and Norc."

"You gotta hook me up with some of that." Deirdre considered that Vic, Perc, Ox and Norc referred to Vicodent, Percocet, OxyContin and Norco.

Deirdre heard the steel door open, keys jingling and footsteps. Deirdre sucked in her breath.

The guard casually walked by Deirdre's cell without even a glance. Deirdre's shoulders slumped as she let out her breath. The pale, cold walls stared back at her as if mocking her; a grim reminder of her insignificance.

Cancel. Cancel. Deirdre visually erased those dreary thoughts. *I really don't want attention.*

Clank, clank, clank. Deirdre turned to see the guard knocking on CeeCee's cell door with her night stick. "Your lawyer's here." The guard unlocked CeeCee's cell, handcuffed her and led her into the hallway.

Deirdre watched as the guard and CeeCee chit-chatted as they walked down the hallway.

As the guard passed Deirdre's cell, she turned to address Deirdre, "You're next, Morgan. Your lawyer just arrived." A slight smile formed at the guard's outer lips.

Deirdre opened her mouth and started to ask a question, but it was too late. Watching CeeCee and the guard waltz past her cell as if they were two school girls chatting in the school hallway, left Deirdre speechless.

Jingle, click, turn, release, door open and shut. Then silence.

Lights flicker, another click, and darkness!

"Hey," Deirdre walked toward her door and pushed on it. *Still locked.* Deirdre heard a loud buzz and a click, the lights flickered, dimly illuminating the area. Deirdre waited. The formerly eerie silence was replaced with an annoying dull buzz emanating from the orange-hued lights. She went to her cot, plunked down, closed her eyes and tried to sleep.

She awoke to the familiar sound of the guard's footsteps. Within minutes Deirdre was sitting across from Marcy, the *Daily Sun* corporate lawyer in the County jail's interview room. The pale green walls of the 20' by 20' room reminded Deirdre of her 1st grade classroom. Bright fluorescent lights – one that flickers, which in 1st grade was a welcome distraction, because it meant that the school janitor and his trusty ladder would disrupt the lesson to change the bulb.

Marcy looked out of place seated on the cracked plastic chair across the table from Deirdre. She tried to keep the sleeves of her tailored, deep blue Armani suit from touching the matching plastic table.

"Change of plan, huh?" Deirdre couldn't help but be sarcastic.

"This is ridiculous." Marcy's words were strained. She shifted in her chair and pulled her blonde hair back into a loose ponytail. "Did you know that your fingerprints are on the murder weapon, which is preposterous, considering that we have a solid alibi proving that you were not even near that neighborhood the night of the alleged homicide."

"I know, but I'm not willing to divulge my whereabouts just yet," Deirdre replied.

"I know. We need to keep the drug-trafficking ring investigation under wraps, but this is ..." She paused and looked at Deirdre. "What's it like in there?" Marcy gazed over Deirdre's shoulder, and nodded in the direction of the door leading to the prison cells.

"Well, they don't go over budget on air conditioning that's for sure. And the cleaning service could use something other than bleach. But honestly, it just smells like urine, and there's such an overwhelming feeling of bad energy, ya know?"

"Yeah. I visited Alcatraz when I was a kid, and that's when I understood the word 'eerie.'" Marcy shivered. "The place just gave me the creeps. How about you?"

Deirdre nodded.

Marcy leaned forward. "So, can you stand this place until tomorrow morning? The paper is set to post bail. It stinks that the Judge got called out on emergency. But there's no way around that. Just really poor timing."

Dread grabbed her stomach. "So, I don't *really* have a choice. I just wish I could get something to write with and keep notes. Or, something to read."

"I know. I tried to bring you a book, but they said that was contraband.

Deirdre sighed.

"Oh, yeah, and the boss wants you to think about writing something like 'My night in prison.' He says it will keep your mind off of your current surroundings. Plus, it will help publicize this incident."

"And sell papers."

"Yes, of course." Marcy smiled. "Could be a front-page article." Marcy spoke with enthusiasm, using her hands to animate. When she accidentally brushed her arm against the table, her eyes widened and she jerked her arm away from the surface.

Deirdre laughed. "Marcy, you need to get out of here. Could you do one other thing for me?"

"What is it?" Marcy sat restrained.

"Please call Grand Master Kim and let him know why I won't be at class to teach this evening. Give my apologies." Deirdre shrugged. "This is unavoidable."

"Sure, I'll call. I'm sure he'll understand."

Deirdre contemplated as she looked down at the plastic table. "I'll explain what I can to him later." Deirdre wrung her hands, then drummed them on the table. "Getting arrested doesn't exemplify the tenets of Tae Kwon Do." Deirdre massaged her temples, looked up and then motioned to the guard who approached her with handcuffs at the ready.

Deirdre stood. "Marcy, thanks for visiting and bringing me the good news as well as something to keep my mind occupied for the rest of the evening."

"Do those hurt?" Marcy winced as the guard locked the cuffs.

"Not unless I tighten real hard," the guard responded.

Deirdre smiled at Marcy. "Which she won't." Deirdre hoped.

CeeCee and her lawyer huddled together at a grey plastic table near the corner of the room. The guard and Deirdre moved toward the door and then walked down the hallway. As

Deirdre entered her cell, the guard unlocked Deirdre's wrists and handed her a piece of paper.

The guard smiled. "This note's for you, but you didn't get it from me."

"Thanks." Deirdre closed her fist around the note.

The guard turned, closed and locked the door. Deirdre's hands shook as she rushed to read the note. *Strange acquaintances prison makes,* Deirdre thought. *I believe I have more than a front-page headline.* She smiled to herself. *Interesting how one chance encounter could be key to helping me expose the truth about Councilwoman Janice Tyler.*

* * *

"What d'ya think?" Mike chomped on a mouthful of gum and intently studied the road ahead. It was just past 4:30 in the morning, and they were headed back to San Antonio to report on their meeting with Detective Maldonado.

"What did I think?" Stuart noted Mike's attempt to appear calm. "I think we've got more than a homicide in San Antonio!" Stuart reached for the manila folder resting on the floorboard in front of him. He shuffled through and read from one of the papers: "Observation. The prescription drugs are traced to a health facility in San Antonio. The origins have been narrowed down to several physicians at the facility who frequently prescribe these drugs. This is no implication of the physicians. We suspect that the drugs are being diverted illegally."

They discussed the case, reading through files until six o'clock in the morning. Mike pulled off Exit #524 for breakfast at a fast-food restaurant.

The car radio blasted. "This is WOAI. We bring you news every hour on the hour. Up next, *Daily Sun* attorney Marcy Cavarino will discuss why reporter Deirdre Morgan spent the night in prison. According to Cavarino, Morgan will be released on bail after a 9 a.m. bail hearing today. And Morgan's article about her night in prison will appear in the *Daily Sun* later this week."

"Did you hear that!" Stuart hastily tapped Mike's arm. Stuart turned to him, but Mike was staring intently into the bag of food he'd just received from the drive-thru window.

"Stuart. Ummm, is this a burger joint? Or are we getting a breakfast burger and a joint?"

"Huh?" Mike held the bag open to display its contents to Stuart.

Stuart looked and held up his hands. He didn't want to touch anything. "I guess our drive-thru stop just turned into a bust." Stuart pulled out his telephone and dialed the local police. "This is Detective Beaumont from the San Antonio Police Department, can I talk to the Chief?"

The drug bust proved useful. The perps were frightened high school students who talked a lot and had no qualms about giving out names, descriptions and information about their supplier. Stuart and Mike got a lead on a San Antonio connection.

Stuart glanced at his watch as he and Mike continued their drive back to San Antonio. The incident only delayed their arrival in San Antonio by one hour.

"Mike, I want you to drop me off at the county jail. I need to be there by 9 a.m."

Mike drummed his fingers on the steering wheel. "Are you gonna tell her ... about your dad?"

"I doubt she'll want to talk *about* me at all, maybe *at* me." He paused. "Besides, it's history."

"Is it?"

"I was a graduate, fresh out of the Criminal Justice school when Dad died. He helped pay for my college education. All those years. All that knowledge and training that he paid for me to have, when he was the one who needed it. I wish I would've taken time off to be with him or taken him out to the shooting range. Just a few times so he would know how to handle a gun. That may have saved his life."

Mike coughed into his hand. "C'mon, L.G., your dad wouldn't have wanted you to take time off from your new job to babysit him. He chose to be unarmed. That's just the way he was. He didn't like guns or the violence that went with them."

Stuart rubbed his palms across his thighs. "My dad was crazy with that newspaper business of his ... 'always seek truth and justice.' Those were his famous words. And nearly his last.

There he was, lying in the hospital bed, seventy-five percent of his body crushed by the printing press. An *accident* they say, that occurred one day after *The Glenbrook News* exposed the connection between the county sheriff department's involvement in a cover-up of the sheriff's wife's murder. And he still wants to 'seek truth and justice.'" Stuart shook his head. "Not without a weapon. Not without training, street smarts and good, solid self-defense."

Mike kept his eyes on the road ahead of him. "You're not to blame for your mom's sadness or your father's death. He knew what he was getting into. He made choices, and he did what he believed in."

CHAPTER EIGHT

Letty was ten minutes early for her volunteer shift at the hospital. She walked toward the nurse's station located in the center of the Geriatric wing. She saw her volunteer shift partner Dolores, an elderly woman who had volunteered at the hospital for four years since her late husband passed.

"Hi, Dolores. How is everyone doing this morning?"

Dolores turned to face Letty. Dolores wrinkled her brow and her lips were drawn tight. "Awake and grouchy." She moved her hands up in the air. "And poor Mr. Brown in Room 309. You know, he is the sweetest man."

"Yes." Letty smiled. "Mr. Brown always has something kind to say."

"Well, not so much anymore." Dolores shook her head and clenched her hands together. She turned her attention to a tray of paper cups that she was filling with juice. She started lining the cups neatly in rows. "He says he's in pain during the night and early morning. He's asked me to ask the doctor to give him some other pain medicine or increase his pain medicine or just please do something so he can sleep, he said. Bless his soul."

"Hmmm." Letty wondered. "Was there a full moon last night?"

"I don't think so. But it sure does seem like it. You know, Nurse Hutchins says it's always crazy during a full moon. But there was no full moon last night. Just a floor full of not-so-happy patients."

Letty watched as Dr. LeMonroe, a young physician who had a great rapport with the patients, headed toward the nurses' station. He glanced at his watch.

"Who's the charge nurse on the floor, and is she here now?" Dr. LeMonroe asked.

"Nurse Hutchins," Letty quickly replied. "And, yes, she's here now. She's training a new nurse and is in with Mrs. Weigand, Room 307. Can I help you?"

Dr. LeMonroe tapped his pen against his clipboard. He looked irritated. "No. Can you just let her know that I need to see her this morning? It's important. I'm starting my rounds now, so I'll be here for at least an hour." He walked away before Letty or Dolores had time to answer.

Letty turned to Dolores. "What do you think that was about?"

"I don't know, but he didn't look too pleased. I hope everything is okay with Nurse Hutchins. She works so hard." She hesitated and raised her brow. "Speaking of hard-working nurses. I heard about Nurse Hayden's husband." She gave Letty a side glance. "Murdered? Can you believe that?" Dolores put her hands in the air. "Sounds like they found the killer. I heard it on the news early this morning. That just puts a new twist on the girl next door." Dolores winked at Letty and smiled. "I tell you there are just strange things happenin' all over this city."

Letty nodded in agreement, and turned to help Dolores line up the cups and continue filling them. "It's a scary, scary thing, Dolores." She made sure the cups were neatly aligned and turned each seam so each lined up uniformly. "I used to feel so safe in my neighborhood. And poor Charlene." Letty stopped and placed a hand on Dolores' shoulder. "But don't you believe everything you hear on the news, Dolores. I just can't believe Deirdre Morgan would do such a thing."

Dolores didn't miss a beat. "Well, I heard it on the news, so it must be right." She started placing cups on her individual tray.

"We'll see. I think even news reporters make mistakes."

Letty and Dolores each took a tray of drinks, placed them on a cart, and began distributing them to each of the patients who were awake.

As Letty approached Mrs. Weigand's room, she noticed Dr. LeMonroe approaching.

He stepped in front of Letty. “Excuse Me,” he said as he opened the door. “After you.”

Letty smiled. “Thank you.”

Nurse Hutchins turned to look at Letty and Dr. LeMonroe as they entered the room.

“Good morning, Mrs. Wiegand,” Dr. LeMonroe addressed the patient.

Mrs. Wiegand, who was receiving her oxygen, could not talk easily. She nodded and smiled through the clear mask that was strapped loosely beneath the bridge of her nose and covered her mouth.

“Can I have a minute with you, Nurse Hutchins?” Dr. LeMonroe’s smile was strained.

“Yes, doctor.” Nurse Hutchins quickly stood. She and Dr. LeMonroe left the room.

Letty let her mind wander as she thought about the handsome Dr. LeMonroe.

Letty had never married.

“You’re so stupid. How could you ever expect any man to love you? You are so lucky to have me.” Her father’s daily reminders to Letty’s mom still made Letty shudder.

Lucky to have you. Right!

Letty’s mom’s life was filled with cowering to please her father in hopes of gaining a compliment. In the end, Letty’s mom welcomed his silence.

Letty vowed to never let her mother’s life become hers.

“You’re so smart,” she remembered her mother telling her. “Study hard. Get good grades. Don’t settle for anything but the best – A’s and hundreds. You can do it.”

So she did. Letty made straight A’s through high school, landing her admittance to a prestigious private university in San Antonio.

While there, she dated and fell in love. Brian was a foreign-exchange student. He earned a full scholarship to the university’s well-respected engineering school. He led Letty into the world of romance, and, for once, she felt like a woman.

As their dating became more serious, so did her parents' threats to stop paying Letty's tuition.

"He is not good enough for you." Her mother pleaded.

"You can't trust foreigners." Her father insisted.

Letty's love for Brian was strong, but the stakes were high.

"Letty. I love you. Why are you doing this?" Brian's words still stabbed at Letty. She'd buried the feelings in a place where no one could penetrate and nothing could escape.

"I just need a little more time to myself and to devote to my studies," Letty lied. She had to fight the urge to embrace him and cling to him, beg him not to let her go.

Her insistence was stronger than his pleading. And that day something died deep within Letty's heart.

Letty's high grades conveniently disguised her emotional lows. Bible study class, prayer and romance were replaced with a renewed relationship with her tear-stained pillow and a courtship with self-disdain.

College life felt just like home.

After college graduation, Letty moved back in with her parents. She spent hours in the backyard garden, turning her passion for plants and flowers into an award-winning hobby. Through the years, she also cared for her parents. About seven years ago, her father died in his sleep. After his death, Letty and her mother became active in the local botanical society, and Letty's love for gardening blossomed. About three years ago, Letty's mother began slowly degenerating with Alzheimer's disease. Within a few months, she also suffered a mild stroke and was hospitalized. She died of pneumonia and other complications.

Letty became a volunteer at the hospital where she had spent those last days with her mother.

The phone rang and brought her back from her musings. She returned the drink cart to the central station, grabbed a stapler and headed towards the floor's central bulletin board.

Letty posted notes and photos on the bulletin board near Nurse Hutchins' office. She tried not to be too obvious as she observed the meeting between Dr. LeMonroe and Nurse Hutchins in the 12' x 10' office encased by floor-to-ceiling clear glass. The door was closed, blocking any sounds, but their actions told a story.

Dr. LeMonroe held a patient chart open on the desk. Nurse Hutchins turned to open the credenza behind her desk and pulled out a file. She was pointing to some items on a paper in the file, and writing a list. He closed the file. She folded her hands on her desk and addressed him. She looked concerned. Shortly after, Dr. LeMonroe rose and began to approach the door.

Letty studied the bulletin board and arranged items. As she heard Dr. LeMonroe's footsteps fade away, she heard the rising sound of Dolores' footsteps and the wheels of the drink cart from behind her. Letty turned to see Dr. LeMonroe enter Mr. Brown's room. And then she turned to Dolores.

"That looks good." Dolores praised Letty's work on the bulletin board.

"It was long overdue for an update." Letty stepped back to observe her work and then turned to join Dolores. The two walked toward the central station.

From the corner of her eye, Letty could see that Nurse Hutchins remained in her office.

"What do you think that was about?" Letty whispered to Dolores as they began lining up cups again for another round of drinks.

"I dunno. But it's sure to keep Nurse Hutchins here late tonight. You know how she is. 'Don't put off 'til tomorrow what can be done today. Because there will be a whole new set of problems tomorrow.' That's her motto."

"Now I do know one thing." Dolores pointed one of her knotted, crooked fingers towards the ceiling as she continued. "That this floor has been a grouchy floor on and off for the past few months. And it didn't use to be that way. No, sirreee. There were the usual moans and groans and you know there's always a talker in one of the rooms, but this is something else. Now some may blame it on the full moon or whatever," Dolores was talking with her hands. "But it may be something that that cute Dr. LeMonroe has seen or heard. And you know him. He'll get to the bottom of it. Yes, sirree. You can bet your bottom dollar on that."

"That's so true," Letty nodded. "Whatever it is, between Doc LeMonroe and Nurse Hutchins, they will find a way to make it right." Letty wondered whether Charlene Hayden worked last night. And Letty needed to return Deirdre's gold Tae Kwon Do necklace.

* * *

Nurse Hutchins studied the patient files. She was no stranger to drug diversion, the use of prescription drugs for recreational purposes. A growing challenge in the healthcare industry, it accounts for a majority of prescription drug abuse and plenty of work for the U.S Drug Enforcement Administration. Recent mandates included a stringent tracking process for controlled-drug dispensing, requiring proof of identification for certain prescription drugs, and banning generic forms of opioid drugs, such as OxyContin, because of the poor tracking methods.

Nurse Hutchins reviewed the files again. She would stay late and discuss this with the charge nurse at night. Together, they'd find the source. She closed the file, grabbed a pad of paper and a pen, and pushed back in her chair. Time to visit the patients.

As she left her office, she noticed the brightly colored, updated bulletin board in the hallway. *Nice work. I'll have to remember to watch the volunteers. Everyone is a suspect.*

She knocked on Room 309.

"Hi, Mr. Brown, I'm Nurse Hutchins."

"I know who you are," his voice was gruff. He glanced to the side and looked at his hands.

"Of course, you do. I was just trying to mind my manners." She smiled and sat beside Mr. Brown's bed.

Nurse Hutchins noticed the ends of Mr. Brown's lips curl into a smile. "Well, that's all right."

"Mr. Brown, we're doing a survey of how well we're doing with pain management, and I'd like to ask you a few questions. It states here that you requested additional pain medication last night at about ten, did that help?

"I didn't request any extra pain medication last night. The nurse brought me my two pills at nine o'clock, like always."

Nurse Hutchins made notes on her pad. “Hmmm. Are you sure?”

“Yes, absolutely.”

Nurse Hutchins shifted in her chair. “With that aside. How would you rate your comfort level, with one being poor and ten being great?”

“About a three – on a good day.”

“Okay, and was there a time when it was better or worse than a three?”

“Yes, it used to be in the nine to ten range, up until about three months ago. Then it went downhill ... fast. I can’t sleep at night because of the pain. And the nurse brings me two pills. But that doesn’t really help.”

“I see. I’m sorry to hear that, Mr. Brown. I will make a note on your chart, and confirm that you are to receive your prescribed medication before bedtime. Let’s see if that makes you more comfortable. Does that sound good?”

“I appreciate that. Anything that will help me fall asleep will be an improvement.” Mr. Brown dropped his hands to the side of his bed.

“Okay, I’ll go check on that now, so you can count on a good night’s rest this evening.” Nurse Hutchins patted Mr. Brown’s hand as she pushed back her chair and stood. “Is there anything else I can do for you?”

“If you could turn off the light. All this talk about sleep has made me drowsy.” He rested his head on the pillow.

Nurse Hutchins turned off the light. “Sweet dreams,” she whispered. She turned and left Room 309.

CHAPTER NINE

At 9 a.m. Wednesday, Deirdre was led into the courtroom. Bond was set at $200,000. Marcy was there to post bond for Deirdre's release.

Deirdre exited the courtroom, and went to reclaim her personal items. She entered the small room where she had first been escorted into yesterday.

The female officer behind the counter looked at Deirdre. "Your personal items are in Interrogation Room 3," and the officer directed her towards the room.

Deirdre cautiously entered, where she faced Detective Stuart Beaumont, who was sitting at the only table in the room. In the center of the table was the unopened box that contained Deirdre's personal items.

"Good morning," Stuart said. Deirdre caught a glimpse of what she perceived as guilt in his eyes.

"Good?! It would be good if I were waking up in my own bed!" Deirdre retorted as she walked towards the table to gather her personal items. She was all too aware that she had no makeup on, and her hair was not well coiffed.

"You knew there were risks going into this job," Stuart looked down at his hands. He paused. "I do apologize though. There were complications." His words lingered. "I didn't know until this morning." He cleared his throat. "But you did sign up for this job, and the Chief is grateful."

Deirdre was silent. She shifted her weight and crossed her arms across her chest.

"I am a professional. So, when I tell someone that I will do something, I do it. No excuses. No anything. Of course, I will continue to hold up my part of the deal, even though you have failed miserably in yours." Deirdre noticed that Stuart's mouth started to open as if to say something. She held up her hand.

"Don't ever expect me to take *you* at *your* word again! I'm going home now. Give the Chief my regards." Deirdre angrily reached for the box.

Stuart grabbed her wrist, holding it firmly. "Please let me explain." Deirdre noticed the pleading look in his eyes. "Judge Bailey was called away on a family emergency. He is the only judge privy to the information about you, and the only one who could set bail for you. It was too risky to tell Judge Weber about the set up. So we had to wait for Judge Bailey."

"Why couldn't you tell Judge Weber?" Deirdre pulled her wrist away. It was warm where he held it.

"Because it might be too risky."

"Oh, is he not trustworthy?" she asked.

"Not trustworthy? What?" Stuart sounded confused. He pulled back, stood and held a chair for her, as if waiting for her to be seated.

She hesitated, and then settled into the chair. "Anything new on the case?" Deirdre wanted to know, and she wanted to be sure that anything she had to do with Detective Stuart Beaumont was strictly business. She rubbed her wrist.

"Nothing to share right now. Most of it is still being held confidential." Stuart sat down.

"Confidential? You know, Detective Beaumont, I'm not in the mood for you to withhold information or have a pompous attitude." Deirdre pounded her fist onto the table. "While you sit here carrying a gun, thinking you're making a difference. You're not." Deirdre's hands pressed into the table. She felt her heart beating faster and tightness in her chest. Her voice became louder. "All you're doing is keeping wayward teenage punks off the street. You should leave the real investigative work to us 'big girls with the pens and paper.'" Deirdre was anxious to let her publisher and Curtis know about the new acquaintance she had made in prison.

"Really!" You've got to be kidding. Reporters have no rules to live by and no integrity to team with it. They'll sell their mothers or throw a friend 'under the bus' for a good story, and they don't bother to check the facts until way *after* the article is printed. Reporters have no scruples – they don't care about whose lives they ruin. And you ... you have no responsibility to keep our streets safe."

"What?! I do have that responsibility, and what I do makes a difference ... a big difference. Your badge and gun don't keep our streets safe."

"Admit it. You just want a byline, headlines on the front page and journalism awards so you can get your picture on the wall of fame."

Deirdre moved to the edge of her chair. "If it weren't for the news, you'd have no hero's glory. Your badge and gun only have impact because people see the good cops busting the bad guys on the nightly news. Thanks to the media, we give people the perception that police officers are keeping the streets safe. In reality, the badges are used to badger as much as they are to bust."

"I don't think you mean that or even believe that." Stuart leaned back in his chair. She watched his hands as he brought them to rest on his thighs. As Stuart's eyes met hers, Deirdre noticed his face soften. "Look, there's always going to be cops who 'badger' as you say ... even cops on the take. Just like there are reporters on the take. And politicians on the take who 'sell out' in order to get good news coverage or escalate their careers, their family's status in the city, whatever." Stuart opened his arms and turned his palms upwards. "And they are livin' large."

"And they're living a lie!" Deirdre pushed back in her chair.

"That's how you see it. And I see it that way, too. But I think these people actually justify their actions. They tell themselves 'everyone's doing this.'"

"No kidding." Deirdre nodded and waved her hands in front of her to accentuate her words. "I sat in a board meeting here in Bexar County where the longtime board member actually said out loud – 'Well, everyone fudges on their taxes. Even the Kennedys fudged on their taxes. It's okay ...' I couldn't believe it." Deirdre put her hands in her lap and looked straight ahead. "At least in the Midwest, they try to hide it. They at least try to portray a reputable cover. Here, they just put it out there."

"Right. There's 'big brother.' And that's the attitude that gets folks into trouble." Stuart rested his arms on the table.

"And a great sense of entitlement."

"That, too. And the attitude of criminals is interesting. I've seen teenagers get into trouble for stealing, but with many different intentions. I had one kid, who was an auto thief, and he was small and agile and fast, so he was good at it, but we finally caught him. When we went to court to testify, the mother was in the back of the courtroom in tears, wailing." Stuart pulled his hands off the table and threw them out in front of his chest. "Her son's parole officer tried to console her and say that juvenile facility would be good for him. Do you know what she told him?"

Deirdre gasped, touched Stuart's arm and held her hand to her mouth. "Are you referring to the Alarcon trial?"

Stuart balled his hands into fists and deliberately dropped them onto the table, his fists banging. "Yes, that one." He looked at Deirdre. "I remember. You were there, and your news buddies were brutal on the SAPD."

"Well, y'all were brutal on that 13-year-old, first-time offender." She threw her body forward and grasped the edge of the table. "No leniency. No breaks for the kid, just send him off to juvey!"

Stuart leaned back in his chair and rested his hands on his knees. "Deirdre, you don't know the half of it. But do you know what his mother told the parole officer?"

"What?" Deirdre folded her arms across her chest.

"Auto theft was how the family survived financially, and he was the best at it. So, with her teenage son in juvey, how would her family survive? That's what she was worried about."

"So, counseling or family therapy might have been in order ... job training." Deirdre leaned forward, nearly banging her knees on the lower side of the table.

"Deirdre," Stuart held up his palms, shaking his head. "You don't know the half of it."

"I'm listening." Deirdre sat up straight, squared her shoulders and clasped her hands in front of her. "You have my full attention."

Stuart rested one of his hands on hers. His voice softened. "Deirdre, there are some things that I just can't tell you."

Deirdre pulled her hands away. She closed her lips tightly.

Stuart rested his hands on the table. "Will you just listen, please?" He didn't wait for a response. "Then there are kids from the other side of the tracks. Who are wealthy and their parents buy them everything, but they break into cars because they're bored, or they just wanted to see if they could do it. Now, I gotta tell you. It's the same crime, but under totally different circumstances. And who do you think gets off easier, because they have better lawyers? But truly, the kids who are breaking into cars for sport are probably more delinquent than the ones who are doing it for survival."

"And the so-called public servants who are motivated by greed, selfishness and ego, or just trying to prove that they can put a teenage kid in jail. They are even worse." Deirdre felt Stuart's eyes search her face.

His voice was gentle. "Deirdre, we've got enough to contend with on the streets." She sensed his sincerity. "We are the good guys."

"We nothing. I am not part of the *we* you are talking about." She clenched her jaw.

Stuart pulled at a corner of the box on the table. "Yes, Deirdre, you are. I believe that you *and I* do the right thing, even if it sometimes appears to be wrong."

Deirdre grabbed at the box that Stuart was toying with and yanked it away from his hands. "Explain! Explain how your very harsh testimony of that 13-year-old boy was in any way doing the right thing."

Deirdre noticed Stuart's shoulders slump forward. "Deirdre, do you promise not to breathe a word of what I'm about to tell you?"

She nodded.

"The Alarcon boy begged us to be harsh on him. He *wanted* to go into juvey."

Deirdre slapped her hand on the table. "Yeah, right."

Stuart held Deirdre's wrist and met her gaze. "The things that his father and uncle were doing to him ... physically, mentally ... it was brutal. They had been abusing him since he was about 3 years old. He wanted out. He wanted to be anywhere and go anywhere but back home, back to what he called his 'personal torture chamber.'" Stuart loosened his hold and let out a sigh. He pulled back in his chair. Deirdre noticed a near pleading in his eyes. "I don't see any point in us arguing about any of this." He stared across the room.

Deirdre was speechless for a moment. "I knew there was something strange going on there – my gut told me to stop covering the story..."

"The Chief noticed – that you lightened up on the department. Actually stopped covering the story altogether."

Deirdre continued "...especially when the mother started hosting fundraisers for her son's appeal." Deirdre looked at Stuart, who was now staring down at his hands. "And then Mrs. Alarcon started driving around town in a new car. She had new clothes for each press conference, and started hanging out at medi-spas and fancy restaurants. But she never visited her son in juvey." Deirdre's voice trailed off.

"It's like Tonto and the Lone Ranger." Stuart's lighthearted remark jolted Deirdre's thoughts back to the present.

Deirdre lowered her hands. "Speaking of Tonto and the Lone Ranger, they *did* share information. So is there anything new on the case?" Deirdre changed the subject.

"There is something that we found that may be of interest."

"Go on," she waited.

"A prescription form from Fairlane Hospital. The officer who secured the crime scene found it outside of the Hayden house on the side lawn." Stuart pulled his chair forward, straight across from and closer to Deirdre.

"Is it dated? Is there a name on it? What dr—"

"Yes, it's dated for Sunday. The *homicide* Sunday."

"Have you questioned Charlene?"

"Yes. Actually, she's the one who mentioned it first. When she gave us her statement."

"You know she's a nurse at Fairlane Hospital? The Geriatric floor."

"Yes, I know. She said she was working the midnight shift Sunday night and Monday morning. We have eyewitnesses who can verify her whereabouts," Stuart placed his hands on the table. "Anyway, when she came home early Monday morning, she said she was carrying her lab coat and had dropped the coat due to the wind. She said: 'there's probably stuff from my pockets all over, tissues, old prescription forms, who knows what else.' It's all in a report that I will bring to you later."

"Hmmm," Deirdre paused and looked toward the door. "Can I get a copy of that prescription form?" Deirdre turned and looked Stuart in his eyes. "I did spend the night in jail and all."

"Consider it done. But why?"

Deirdre shifted in her chair. She smiled. "Just curious. Most medicines at the hospital are distributed using an automated, pre-set dose dispenser. Most hospitals use a Scripto. So, why would Charlene have a prescription form?"

"We considered that. But other nurses say that happens every so often. They say they've even left work with morphine in their pockets. They dispense medicine, or carry a patient's prescription form down to the pharmacy lab in the hospital, and sometimes they just take the form back," Stuart defended.

"I see," Deirdre answered, but she didn't buy it.

"Okay, Deirdre. What are you thinking?"

"Nothing." She rubbed her temples. "I need some rest."

"Look, don't you go getting any ideas about doing Private I. work, okay? Just write the reports for the Chief." He leaned forward. "Are you listening?"

"Of course. Yes, sir," she said as she crossed her left leg over the right and leaned her body away from him.

Stuart saw that look of determination in Deirdre's eyes and wished that she weren't involved in this case at all. It wasn't safe.

"Deirdre," he looked into her eyes. This was the first time he had seen her without makeup. He wanted to capture the portrait of her face, the soft white skin that surrounded her eyes, the well-defined, pouted lips, the very light freckles neatly painted onto her nose and cheeks, and those almond-shaped, emerald-green eyes, highlighted by her dark brown medium-length eyelashes. When she smiled, he noticed how her eyes lit up.

"Curtis drove your car over here from your office. He said he knew where you kept the spare key. I want you to please drive directly home and get that needed rest. You still have my cell phone number and the card I gave you, right?"

"Yes," she answered.

"Okay, once you get inside and settled, please look around the inside and outside of your house, and let me know if anything has been moved or is different, okay?"

"Right."

Deirdre exited the prison and was surrounded by reporters. She stopped to address them.

"You can read my comments in the *Daily Sun*. My investigation will reveal the true murderer in this case. Thank you." She headed toward her car. The smooth leather seats beneath her felt soft and plush. She grasped the steering wheel and smiled. Freedom coupled with a good investigation was invigorating.

As Deirdre approached her house, she stopped at her decorative stone mailbox near the driveway. She pulled the mail out and glanced at one of the envelopes. A shiver went up her spine. Her fingers began to tremble and she gasped for air. The envelope dropped to her lap.

CHAPTER TEN

The incessant tone of the telephone awakened Letty from her dream. Without lifting her eye mask, she reached for the phone.

She answered with a barely audible, "Hello."

"Did you return it?"

"Yeah."

"You wore the gloves?"

Letty sucked saliva through her teeth. "Yeah."

"So you know what to do now, right?"

"Not really." Letty lifted off her eye mask and sat up in bed. "Hey, I have to ask you something. Did you—"

"I gotta go. I'll touch base with you later."

"Hey."

"When do I get my cut?"

"Soon."

Letty pulled at her bed sheet. "That's what you said two weeks ago. I need something *now*."

I'll see what I can do and get back to you soon—"

"What?"

"If my contact's there, I can have an answer in ten minutes."

Letty clamped her hand tight around the phone. "I'll give you ten minutes. That's all."

"How's the handsome Captain doing? Have you talked to him lately?"

Letty loosened her grip on the bed sheet. “Okay, get back to me when you can.”

“Thought so.” *Click. Tone.*

* * *

“Murderer.” The large, cursive letters were scribbled in blood-red ink across the white envelope.

Deirdre took a deep breath. “Well, that certainly is report-worthy.” Deirdre gathered her thoughts.

She drove past her emptied, upside down garbage can, drove her car up into her driveway, put it in park, and studied the handwriting. She turned off the car’s ignition. The word was centered on the envelope. No address. Someone had placed it in her mailbox.

She stepped out of her midnight blue Lexus, gripped her garbage can, and proceeded towards her front door. The mat at the front of her house read: “Home Sweet Home.” She couldn’t have agreed more.

As she placed her key in the front door, she heard her phone ringing. She rushed inside and answered it.

“Hello.”

“Deirdre, how are you?” Curtis’ voice greeted her.

“Oh, hi, Curtis! I’m exhausted. I’m going to take a long, hot bubble bath and then work on some notes from home.”

“Well, don’t make that bath too long. I’ve got a very interesting message for you.”

“Oh, really?”

“Yes. It’s from CeeCee. She left the message with the receptionist. ‘Let’s get together soon. Call me.’ Isn’t that Reeks’ girlfriend? What’s up with that?”

“I met her during my little prison gig. She said she would call, but I didn’t think it would be that fast. Or that she knew that I worked at the newspaper.”

“Well, she called at ten this morning. But what’s going on? Why is she calling you?

“Curtis, Cee Cee was in the county jail yesterday, too. We talked a bit, and she left me her number. We didn’t talk too long, but I managed to get the point across that I was interested in some of her *goods*."

There was a long pause on the other end of the telephone line.

"Oh, wow. Are you sure about this?"

"I figure the more evidence and the more information we get, the better. We can get a tape recording —"

"Deirdre," Curtis interjected. "It's too dangerous. There must be another way without you getting involved in any more undercover work."

"Maybe you're right, but it seems like a great lead. Think about it. We'd need to work this together somehow."

"Okay. I'll think about it. In the meantime, Joe, Marcy and I are concerned about your safety. So much that they put us on city council meeting duty tomorrow morning. That's why I'm calling. I wanted to see if you're up to it."

"Councilwoman Tyler will be there, right?"

"She has items on the agenda. That minimum security prison."

"Oh, perfect." Deirdre paused. "What time is the meeting?"

"Nine o'clock. Do you think you'll be in before then, or should we just meet at council chambers?"

"Let's meet at council chambers. I really need a long bubble bath and a good night's rest after my jailhouse stay."

"That's fine. I'll let Joe and Marcy know that you're up for covering the meeting."

"Thanks." Deirdre hung up the phone.

She ascended her stairway. At the top of the stairs, she took a brief detour before entering her bedroom. She turned to her left, where she selected a thick bath towel from the floral sachet-scented linen closet. She gently placed the towel up to her nose and smelled the sweet garden-like aroma left by the sachet she had placed in the linen closet months ago.

She entered her bedroom, chose a book, took out her Smith & Wesson .357 from her nightstand, and went into the bathroom to start her bubble bath.

Deirdre allowed her body to be consumed by the hot water, luxurious bubbles and mineral salts. As she settled back to read her book, she realized that she forgot to mention to Curtis the "murderer" letter she received in the mail. And she needed to include that in her report to the Chief and give it to Detective Stuart Beaumont, so the police could check it for evidence.

"I'll do that later," she thought as she allowed memories of Stuart Beaumont to consume her mind just as the hot bubbles surrounded and massaged her body. She imagined his strong hands, and drifted slowly into sweet dreams.

When Deirdre awoke, the water was bubbleless and tepid. It reminded her of the cold, drab cell she had been in. She exited the bathtub with a chilling shiver. She wouldn't wish that experience on anybody. But at the same time she recalled all of the evil-doers and unconscionable people she had met through her investigative reporting, and knew that the dank, dark cell was better than what they deserved. She wanted to help the police catch the true murderer of Jimmy Lee Hayden and get to the source of the drug traffic ring. She dried off, slipped on her robe, and sat at the corner table where she began to write her observation report notes. Fifteen pages later, she decided to get some much-needed rest. She wanted to have all of her wits about her during tomorrow's City Council meeting.

* * *

At 8:30 a.m., Deirdre pulled into the parking lot near the Municipal Plaza Building at Main and Commerce Streets. When she entered the 1st floor, she noted that the usual media crowd was already there. She spotted Curtis. They entered council chambers and sat together in the front row. At 9 a.m. the meeting began.

Janice Tyler sat in her leather chair within the San Antonio city council chambers. Fellow council members were seated about one foot to each side of her and along the half-circle council desk.

Each of the eight council members had a stationary microphone at his or her seating area. The council members faced the handful of city council meeting visitors before them.

Tyler's gaze appeared fixed on the papers before her. She placed her left hand flat on top of the papers as if marking a place with her fingers. "*Pink dancer. I love that color,*" she thought as she admired her freshly manicured fingernails.

"Councilwoman Tyler. Do you agree?" the Mayor bent forward and turned slightly in his chair, so that he could look directly at her.

Janice Tyler shifted in her chair and pulled her left hand up to her mouth in a loose fist coughing into her hand as she cleared her throat.

"I'm sorry, Mayor. Could you repeat the question? I was reading the report," she lied.

One side of the Mayor's mouth turned slightly upwards as his brown eyes searched Janice Tyler's face for an answer. "The question on the floor is about the redirection of the East Side revitalization project. One that directly affects District 2."

Janice Tyler leaned forward slightly to gain nearer access to the microphone. "Yes, I'm fully aware of that, Mayor," she said as a matter of fact. *Don't' get sassy with me, young boy. I'll take a switch to you like nobody's business.*

"Well, do you agree with the proposed location of the federal minimum security prison? And if so, why, and if not, please explain why not?" The Mayor leaned back in his chair and opened his arms, inviting her response.

Councilwoman Tyler thought she noticed a hint of a glimmer in the Mayor's eyes. "I do agree with the new location."

The Mayor scooted forward to speak directly into his microphone. "Even though it is near a residential housing complex?"

"Yes."

"Could you please explain? My understanding is that you are the voice of your constituents." The Mayor motioned towards the audience.

Councilwoman Tyler noted that several reporters were in the audience. She invited some good press, especially on this controversial topic.

"Yes, I speak wholeheartedly for my constituents on this vital matter. As you know, the East Side revitalization project has had several stuttered starts. We now have the highest crime rate in the city and yet we are within a ten mile radius of one of the federal government's thriving military facilities – Fort Sam Houston. However, the word or talk on the street, if you will, is the same as it has been for decades – 'Don't go over the bridge. That's the bad part of town.'" Janice Tyler paused, and took a sip of water from the clear glass in front of her. "We want to change that. We want to provide safe neighborhoods and good schools for our children, a safe environment for our elderly and positive programs for our youth. To that end, I believe bringing in federal dollars will help establish these safe neighborhoods."

* * *

Janice Tyler grew up on the East Side of San Antonio, near St. Philips College, bordering Walters St., North New Braunfels and near Martin Luther King drive.

Growing up in this high-crime-rate, run-down part of the city, school was Janice Tyler's safe haven. The structure, rules and orderliness appealed to her. Home – well, that was another story. The nights were noisy, littered with shouts, sirens, gunshots and neighbors brawling.

The houses were so close she could hear the intimate, yet loud conversations – usually between 1 a.m. and 4 a.m. – when the local taverns closed shop. She learned quickly to stay away from her house between 8 p.m. and midnight. That was when her mom was making money.

Finally, her mom's sewing business took an upturn and they moved to the near downtown area. That's when Janice Tyler got a taste of the other side of town and learned about hypocrisy.

Her peers in the middle to upper class school would do "pranks" for the fun of it. Stealing to put food on the table seemed more honorable than stealing out of boredom.

Janice decided to take the best of both worlds. As councilwoman and successful entrepreneur, she could have the material wealth of her adolescent peers, but she wanted to make a positive difference in her hometown community.

"Councilwoman Tyler?" Her thoughts were interrupted. "Isn't the proposed site in a high-crime area?" The council member asking the question was the crucial vote that she needed to pass this proposal.

"Yes, which is something we continue to address with the Police Chief. As for the facility, the reasons to build there are twofold. One: it will be the first prison in our area to include public and private security personnel. So, it will provide jobs for local residents who work in or desire to work in the security industry." She cleared her throat and leaned closer to her microphone. "I believe it will encourage our youth to work *outside* of prison bars, rather than find residence inside." Councilwoman Tyler paused. She wanted to be sure the reporters had time to record that quote. "Secondly, I believe we can get federal grants and stimulus funds to develop the now vacant land. So, it will not cost the city, nor will it cost San Antonio residents anything. That's a win-win for everyone."

"I see." The councilmember nodded. "How sure of securing grant money are you? I mean, have you reviewed the requirements? Have you applied for the monies?"

"Yes. I actually have pre-approval on our initial grant request. I didn't include it in the council packets because I thought it'd be best to wait until I receive final approval."

"Thank you." The councilmember leaned forward in his chair. "I motion that we approve this development with the stipulation that the federal grant or stimulus funds are approved and that the building meets all city codes, and compliance and other legal requirements for that land."

"I second that motion," Councilwoman Tyler smiled.

The Mayor leaned forward. "We have a motion on the floor. Clerk can you read the motion?"

"Councilmember Lewis motioned to approve the District 2 land development at Pine Street with the stipulation that the federal grant or stimulus funds are approved and that the building meets all city codes compliance and other legal requirements for that land."

"Thank you." The Mayor smiled. "Is there any discussion?"

All was silent. The council members unanimously approved of the land development.

"This is a milestone for District 2. As you know, it's a project that has been kicked around for over five years. I thank all of the supporters in District 2 who have worked so hard and diligently to make this happen, and I thank my fellow council members for helping to move this landmark development forward." She smiled. A small crowd in the audience clapped and followed with a standing ovation.

* * *

In her office, seated on a luxurious black leather chair behind a large walnut desk, Councilwoman Janice Tyler kicked off her shoes, poured a glass of champagne, and held up her crystal flute.

Her brother-in-law, Vince, and the assistant and office manager, packed in to Tyler's office and poured their own classes of champagne.

Councilwoman Tyler smiled and raised her glass. "To progress."

"Hear! Hear!" The others held up their flutes to mark the occasion.

"Five years, and we finally prevail," Councilwoman Tyler said.

"And so we did," Vince walked to Councilwoman Tyler's chair and stood beside her. He tapped his flute against hers. "I'll drink to that."

"We've covered our bases, right, Vince?" She said softly.

"Covered and buried," Vince grinned and swallowed the remainder of the flute's content.

"Well, all right," Tyler smiled knowingly. "Progress—and a little something for our pocketbooks."

"More than a little, Councilwoman." He drummed his fingers against the empty flute. "Much more than a little." He walked toward the bottle of champagne. "We leased that land for more than five times the purchase price."

"Those stimulus pockets are deep."

"Sure are." He poured champagne into his flute.

"And now, we are *really* in business."

"Land, loot and ludes." He laughed.

"Next is a stadium for the San Antonio Spurs– somewhere here. On the East Side."

"It's all about timing, Councilwoman. All about timing."

"Yes. We can wait until it's right."

"Right on. Once the Spurs win a championship, we push for a public vote to have a stadium on the East Side. No one wants a winning team to leave town." Vince winked at Councilwoman Tyler.

"The world loves a winner." Councilwoman Tyler nodded, and then finished the remainder of her champagne.

CHAPTER ELEVEN

"Meet me at the JC Penney's at North Star Mall," Stuart's voice on the phone sounded quiet and mysterious.

"Where? When?"

"First Floor. Women's purses. 10 a.m." The phone went dead.

Deirdre glanced at the clock radio next to her bed. *7:30 a.m.* She flipped off her cover and sheets, slipped off the bed, put on a robe, and sat at her corner table to finish writing the last pages of her observation report notes. After a call to the office and a quick shower, Deirdre had ten minutes to get to the mall.

As she entered the first floor of Penney's, she went to the purse section and studied one. "Are you finding everything you like?" Stuart's voice was behind her.

"Oh," she was caught off guard. "I didn't even hear you approaching."

"I know. That's why I'm a Detective. I'm paid to pay attention, be aware of my surroundings and observe details."

"Oh, speaking of observing, I have the ..." Deirdre reached into her satchel to grab the report, but Stuart immediately sidetracked her by reaching for her hand. He put it to his lips and kissed it.

Deirdre stilled. "Oh, I see," Deirdre said slowly retracting her hand from his strong, masculine fingers. His eyes lingered on her slender fingers and polished nails.

Stuart's face met Deirdre's. "You need to go ask that gentleman for some help choosing a man's tie," he motioned to a middle-aged sales clerk. "He'll give you complete instructions. I'll talk to you," Stuart said, as he turned and exited the store.

"Hmmmmph," Deirdre sighed. She rubbed the top of her hand where the feel of his warm, full lips lingered. *How would those lips feel against mine?* "Okay, Deirdre, focus. I'm here to help catch the bad guys," she muttered to herself.

Deirdre casually walked up to the tie salesman and listened to his instructions. Deirdre was to go to her car, at which point another gentleman in his own vehicle (a maroon Mercury Cougar) would meet her there, and she was to follow his vehicle to the 'destination point.'

As Deirdre began to drive, she glanced at her car's clock. *10:45 a.m.* She noticed that the gentleman in the Mercury Cougar continually checked his rear view mirror to be sure that Deirdre was close behind.

Twenty minutes later, they pulled into a driveway of a home on the East Side of San Antonio. Deirdre noted the older homes, some in need of repair, some newly renovated to fit the originally constructed historical era of the German settlement times. She entered the one-story home, and directly in front of her was a slate blue couch set in front of a long, ivory-colored wall. Directly to the right was an archway which led to what she assumed was the kitchen. As she looked to her right, she noted the beautiful hardwood floors, covered only by an Oriental area rug. There to her right was Stuart Beaumont, seated at a table near the brick fireplace.

"Is this your office away from home?" she questioned.

"Actually, it is. We do most of our undercover work out of places like this. In the neighborhood, where we believe we can be close to the crime scenes." Stuart paused and cleared his throat. "Speaking of scenes, do you have that report you were so anxious to give me back at Penney's?"

"Yes, here it is," she tossed it across to Stuart, landing it just upon the tabletop.

"Nice throw," he commented as he reached down and opened the report. He read in silence.

Deirdre watched for expressions on his face as he read. There were none until he got to the piece of mail marked "Murderer."

Stuart looked up. "This was in your mailbox?" He held up the envelope that Deirdre had placed in a plastic zipper-lock bag.

"Just someone messing with me. No big deal. It wasn't stamped, so someone put it in my mailbox."

"Or someone may say that you planted it there," he placed the plastic bag aside.

Deirdre crossed her arms. "I didn't even open it."

"I'll send it to the lab for prints and DNA."

Stuart closed the report file. Deirdre was still standing.

"Oh, Deirdre, please sit down. Pardon my manners. Can I get you some tea? Coffee?"

"A cup of tea would be nice," she said as she sat at the table.

"This is a good report." Stuart got up from the table, crossed in front of the fireplace and headed through the archway toward the kitchen.

This is tame compared to the drug-trafficking ring I'm working on, but that's newspaper business, not pro bono police observations. You'd be concerned if you knew about my meeting with CeeCee later tonight, but that's none of your business.

The nearness of Stuart's body as it crossed in front of her brought her back from her musings. "Well, it is my job ... observing and writing." *And doing undercover work.*

"Yes, and you do a good job at that, too, so I'm told." Deirdre watched as he filled the tea kettle with water and set it on top of one of the stove's burners.

"You've never read my articles?"

"When I read the paper, I read the articles, and don't necessarily pay attention to who writes them."

"So much for observant," Deirdre said under her breath.

"What kind of tea would you like, Deirdre?" He stood in the U-shaped archway that separated the kitchen from the front room.

Deirdre felt Stuart's stare and looked up to meet it. "What do you have?"

"Herbal, ginseng, ginger..."

"Ginseng with a little bit of honey would be great," she perked.

Deirdre heard a "Hmmph," from the kitchen.

"If you don't have honey, that's okay." Deirdre responded to the sound.

"Oh, no, I have honey." Deirdre watched as he returned to the call of the whistling tea kettle. She watched the motions of his burly figure in the kitchen as he prepared the tea. He reminded her of a grizzly bear preparing his den, pacing, observing, adjusting. His bear-like stature and gruff composure were clumsily precise.

Stuart burled through the archway and made his way to where Deirdre was sitting. He clutched a black bamboo-handled, oriental design tray on which the two cups of tea, honey, teaspoons and sugar packets were neatly arranged. As he approached the table, Deirdre cleared away the papers.

"Tell me one thing, Deirdre." She felt him study her face. "Why journalism? Why newspaper reporting?" he asked, as he sat down. He emptied two sugar packets into his cup of tea, stirred, wiped the teaspoon clean, and then folded the napkin and placed the teaspoon neatly on the napkin.

"Well, if it's any of your business," she replied curtly, then softened, "I believe in the truth. The truth will set you free. Information is power ... all of those clichés; I believe them and I believe *in* them." Deirdre dipped her teaspoon into the honey jar, stirred it into her cup and haphazardly put the dirty spoon on her napkin.

"Okay, that explains why some journalists do what they do. But why does Deirdre Morgan do what she does?"

"Are you ever satisfied?"

"Yes, when I hear the truth, the whole truth and nothing but the truth." He responded with a half-smile.

"That's exactly what it is." Deirdre enjoyed seeing him relaxed. "The truth. You see, I believe in the truth, and I despise lies. I've seen how lies can destroy innocent people." Deirdre tilted her head to one side and stared directly into Stuart's deep brown, melting-chocolate-like eyes.

"Oh, *now* we're getting somewhere. Tell me about it. How these lies can destroy innocent people." He sat upright in his chair, leaned across the table and placed his elbows on the surface.

"Well, you know lies. Or even half-truths that people justify to get their own way."

"Give me an example."

"Well, take a councilman, for instance."

"Okay."

"Sometimes they sell out."

"Give me specifics."

"Okay. My dad was a city councilman in a Chicago suburb, about twenty miles west of the city. I used to go to council meetings with him."

Stuart nodded.

"Most of the time, they were boring." Deirdre scooted to the edge of her chair. She punctuated her words with her hands. "But there were several controversial votes – like when the city manager recommended purchasing a fire truck that could scale a 20-story building."

"And that was a bad thing?"

"The town's building ordinances restricted buildings to three stories."

"Oh. Did it pass?"

"Yes. Thanks to Marcy's dad."

"You mean Marcy, the lawyer from the *Daily Sun*?"

"One and the same. He and my dad ran on the same ticket, but then he 'went to the other side.' He'd always vote the way the influential contractors, businesses or even the news media favored. If a contractor or business, such as the one selling the over-reaching fire truck, would benefit from the deal, then Marcy's dad would join the ranks and vote for it." She took a quick breath and continued. "There was another time: my dad recommended they adjust the street and school zone speed limit."

"What was the controversy there?

"The street limit was 15 miles per hour and school zone was 20 miles per hour."

"So, drivers would have to speed up in the school zone." The corners of Stuart's mouth formed a smile, and he wrinkled his brow.

"Yeah. That's ridiculous, right?" Deirdre shook her head sideways and looked at the ground. "So, I'd sit and watch and listen during those meetings and the discussions. Then, I'd read about it in our weekly local newspaper. And what occurred at the meeting and what was reported were very different. But it was all very subtle."

"How so?"

"Well, the Village president was easily irritated."

"A hothead?"

"You could say that. He'd raise his voice, make odd, sarcastic comments and cut off discussion from fellow trustees if they had opposing views."

"And how'd that play out in the newspaper?"

"Totally opposite. The city council beat reporter made the guy sound like a saint. Kind, gentle and soft spoken. Just by the subtle use of adjectives. The president 'said' things – those with opposing views were quoted as 'shouting' or 'huffing.'" Deirdre looked up to see Stuart's wrinkled brow and deep brown eyes twinkling. He had a slight curl to his lips. "Really." Deirdre met Stuart's gaze, and she smiled. She lifted her hands to accentuate her point. "The reporter used the word 'huffing.'"

"So, do you have a beef with Marcy because of this history?" Stuart leaned back in his chair and watched Deirdre.

"Well, Marcy's dad did what was politically correct for his own self-interests – he wasn't driven by the need to 'do the right thing.' And Marcy – well, she's cut from the same cloth. So, I don't expect her to hold local public officials accountable for their less-than-honorable behavior. It would be the right thing to do, in my book, but it wouldn't be politically correct for Marcy, if she has public office aspirations of her own, or if the newspaper sees it as more of a risk than a reward."

"So, you want to expose a specific local public official and bring him or her to justice through the media?"

"I simply want to deliver the truth. When we reveal the truth about others, it helps us make informed decisions, and sometimes serves justice." She paused. "When we have a clear view of the truth about ourselves, it helps move us along in our personal journey to become closer to God. You know the phrase, 'the truth will set you free.' I believe that." And Lord knows I repeat that passage from John about God and the Word and it being 'the life and the light of men' over in my head daily.

"Which one?"

"John 1:5 "And the light shineth in darkness; and the darkness comprehended it not."

"He was in the world, and the world was made by him, and the world knew him not." Stuart stared straight ahead as he said, "John 1 –"

"Verse 10." Deirdre looked at Stuart. He stared straight ahead, giving her the chance to soak in the smooth complexion of his skin, interrupted by the shallow lines forming around the corner of his eye and around his lips. His lips were so deeply pigmented and full, she fought the urge to cup her hand around his chin. Instead, with the back of her palm, she gently rested it against her cheek.

Stuart turned and met her gaze. She felt his hand touch her hand.

Deirdre cleared her throat and jerked her hand away. "I guess in our lines of work, we meet a lot of people who can't see the light in the darkness."

"Too many." Stuart dropped his hand onto his knee and rubbed his palm against it. "That's my favorite book in the Bible."

"What is?"

"John. I just like the way he writes. Very plain, yet philosophical. It's like he takes a bird's eye view of things, and then just tells it like he sees it."

"Mmmmm. Yes. That's a good way to put it." Deirdre fidgeted with some papers on the table. John was her favorite book, too. That they shared this taste she found both comforting and disturbing.

Stuart was staring off into the distance. He spoke softly, and Deirdre strained to hear him. "There are graver consequences for speaking the truth than having your name in the paper or losing your job."

"Such as?"

Stuart looked at Deirdre. She felt as if he were searching her face. He rubbed his hands on his thighs, then brought them up to the table, where he clasped them both around his mug.

"Such as anything, Deirdre. Look." He paused and took a sip of tea. "Any time that people, money and power are combined, there's potential for danger. Then you throw in sex, drugs, pride, greed and ego, and that's volatile ... anything and everything is possible." He ran his fingers through his hair and set his hands on the table, looking directly into Deirdre's eyes. "And you need to stay as far away from those volatile situations as possible. That's just the way it is. You've got to let the police do the police work."

Deirdre crossed her arms under her breasts. "Oh, is that right?" she challenged.

Stuart leaned back on his chair, and crossed his arms across his chest. "Yes, that's right."

"Well, let me tell you something, Mr. thinks-he-knows-it-all," Deirdre uncrossed her arms, resting her elbows on the table, but leaving her hands free to emphasize her speech. "I'm the one," she pointed to herself, "who determines what is and is not my business."

"Oh, don't pull this phony, altruistic, duty-to-the-public newspaper stuff with me, Ms. Morgan."

"There is nothing phony about the news and news reporters, Mr. Beaumont." She quickly took a breath. "And what makes you think that your little game of cops and robbers is so great?"

"Oh, so that's the way it is. You resort to name calling, huh?" He leaned forward and spread his hands across the table.

"No, not back to name-calling. Let's just stick with the facts. Okay?" Deirdre rested her arms on the table.

"Sure. The facts."

"The facts are that crime in San Antonio has increased every year since 1988." She held up her hand and began counting out on her fingers. "Drive-by shootings, gang-related killings, drugs on the streets, violence in the schools, and the list goes on." She motioned in the air with her hands. "And response times, they have increased over the years as well. So, if the police can't keep the streets safe, it's up to the media to keep people informed and aware of the dangers on the streets, in their schools and in their neighborhoods. It's up to us news reporters to inform people of how to protect themselves because, in many cases, the police can't respond in time." Deirdre's heart was racing.

"Now you wait one minute." Stuart pushed back in his chair, stood and walked toward the fireplace. "The police do a lot to keep our streets, neighborhoods and schools safe. We catch criminals, arrest them and before you know it, bam!" He clapped his hands together and turned toward Deirdre. "There's a lawyer, and our wonderful court system lets them out on bail or gives a frivolous fine and puts the predators right back on the street so they can claim another victim." He pointed at Deirdre. "That's what you need to be writing about. Not the increased crime rate, but the increased tolerance for criminals to do whatever they want and not be held accountable." He dropped his hands to his side.

"HMMMMPHH!" She slammed the palms of her hands on the table and looked at Stuart. She noticed a red tone in his face. "I am fully aware of problems within the justice system."

"Well, good." He barreled towards the table, gathered up the tablespoons, cups and napkins and tossed them onto the oriental tray. "I'm glad we can agree on that." Deirdre watched as he carried the tray back to the kitchen.

Deirdre sat at the table and pondered. How was she going to find out or use Stuart Beaumont to help her penetrate the possible link in the San Antonio Police Department or within city council to the drugs on the East Side housing projects if she continued to accuse and attack? Why couldn't he understand that she had a job to do? Finding the source of drugs on the East Side was important. Not just to her, but to the police, and to the people in this city.

She put her hands on the table, stood up and walked into the kitchen and began drying the dishes as Stuart finished washing them. "It sounds a bit like we're arguing from the same side. It's just a matter of 'how,' not 'what,'" she said, as she tried to soothe things over.

"Well, the 'how' is a big question. And I just believe that trained and armed professionals should be the ones who catch the bad guys, not innocent, untrained and unarmed people."

"But that's just not the way it is. Innocent people are being attacked every day, and they're beginning to arm themselves and take the necessary precautions to guard their so-called castles ... to protect themselves and their loved ones from injury."

"Don't try to solve the world's problems with the newspaper, Deirdre," his soft voice was a contrast to the zealous way he scrubbed the tea cup. "There's more to solving a crime than publishing the information about the crime. You've got to know that, Deirdre." He stopped scrubbing and looked into her eyes.

Deirdre met his look. She noticed there was almost a pleading, a sea of memories, and she even sensed some pain in that look.

"Why, Stuart? Why is that so important to you?"

"I have my reasons." He placed the tea cup on the drain board.

Deirdre lifted the tea cup and began drying it. "I want to know why, Stuart. Why do you think that journalists don't have what it takes to defend and preserve the truth? Why do you think that only the police can do that? There must be a reason, maybe something personal."

He was zealously cleaning out the sink. He remained silent.

Deirdre continued. "I mean, if we're going to be working together, I should know your emotional triggers."

He stopped scrubbing and let out a short laugh. He looked up at Deirdre and smiled. "My emotional triggers?" he said, shaking the water off of his hands and drying them on the towel Deirdre was holding. "What does that mean?" She noticed a look of curiosity and humor in his eyes. His tone was lighthearted.

Deirdre genuinely liked his smile.

"You know. Things that make you tick, that make your heart beat faster and just trigger some deep-seated emotions." She returned the smile, determined not to let him change the subject. "So, what is it?" She noticed he was still holding the towel.

"What is what?"

"What is it that you don't want to talk about?" She was growing impatient. He tugged at the towel.

"Don't get angry, Deirdre." He folded the towel, and placed it across the front of the sink.

"Fine. I can tell that you don't want to talk about it." She glanced at her watch and noticed that it was nearly 2 p.m. "If we're done with our work here, it's time for me to go." She turned to walk out of the kitchen.

"No, Deirdre, wait," Stuart stammered.

Deirdre turned slightly and faced Stuart.

He wove his hand through the deep black waves of his hair. "You're right. If we're going to work together, we need to know what makes the other tick ... our emotional triggers, as you put it. And I don't want you to go yet. There are a few more points on the case I'd like to share with you."

"And ..." Deirdre crossed her arms.

"Okay, I will tell you about what got me so emotional back there."

"Do you want to sit down?"

"Yes," he said, motioning towards the slate blue couch.

Deirdre sat and waited.

Stuart reclined against the arm of the couch. One leg was propped onto the other. He clasped his hands together against his lips and was silent for a moment as he looked into the fire.

"I knew a great journalist." He stared at the fire. "He owned a group of newspapers in a suburban town in the Midwest. The newspaper was his life." Stuart pressed his fingertips together. "He discovered some key information in a previously unsolved, but high-profile murder case. He made some calls, gathered facts and, wow, it was a doozey. Then, the day after the information came out in the newspaper, he was ..." Stuart paused and looked at the floor.

Deirdre waited. She moved to put her hand on his shoulder, but pulled back.

"Crushed in his own printing press. They said it was an accident, but I never have believed that." Stuart rubbed his eyes with open palms.

"Oh, Stuart," she touched his arm. "And you were very close to this man?"

"Yes," Stuart looked up toward the door. "He was a very, very special man ... a very close friend. He was my father."

Deirdre gently squeezed his arm with one hand and covered her mouth with the other. "Oh, I'm sorry. I'm so sorry." She stammered.

"I knew he was getting into more danger than he could handle. I should have taken some time off to be with him."

"It's really not your fault."

Stuart let his arms slide slightly down his face. Stuart looked at Deirdre's hand on his arm and then looked at Deirdre. "Those words are easy for you to say. You pride yourself on revealing the truth about people and then just walking away. So, you never let anyone down because they know to expect you to be detached. But they expect me to help, to protect and stay with them ... To the end."

Deirdre pulled her arm away.

He shifted his weight, leaned away from Deirdre and continued. "You never see the people whose lives you destroy. You move on to the next story."

Deirdre slapped her arms across her lap. "Is that really what you think?"

Stuart leaned forward. "Well, it's the nature of your business."

"The nature of my business? You make it sound like I'm some database that just sorts, organizes and spits out information. It's more than that. It's emotional. It's ..." Deirdre grabbed some papers and tapped them on her lap. She lined up the pages into a neat, orderly file and placed them neatly onto her lap. "Do you remember the children's story called 'The Emperor's New Clothes'?"

Stuart held his arms open. The corner of his lips curved upwards. "Yes."

"Do you agree that when the emperor has no clothes, someone has to stand out in the crowd and say it?

"Yes."

"Do you think that the little boy in that story did that without risk?"

Stuart scooted forward on the couch. "Well—"

"Do you think that we journalists do that without risk? Without fear of retaliation or backlash?" Her arms kept perfect rhythm with her words. "There is risk, but we're willing to do that so that people can base their lives on a foundation of truth not lies. That's why I do it – to be the one responsible voice in the crowd. And that's probably why your father chose to do it. He didn't want to be saved. He was saving others from the lies and deception of the murderer, the deceiver. That was the only truth he could live ... or die with. Don't you get that? I get that." She ended her sentence by resting her hand on his arm.

Stuart looked at the floor. "I believe that if he would have carried a gun, or had some training in self-defense, he'd still be alive today." He looked up and met Deirdre's gaze. "That's why it's important that you keep a safe distance from this case."

"That may be so." Deirdre was suddenly aware of the strength of his muscles beneath his shirt. She pulled her hand away. "And that's why I do carry a weapon if I'm going into a dangerous situation. I have a license to carry, and I am trained in self-defense."

"You carry a handgun?" He leaned forward on the couch.

"When the situation calls for it, yes." Deirdre brushed her hands across her lap. "You see, Detective Beaumont, there's no need to worry about me. I can take care of myself."

"Even so, I'll watch your back, if that's okay with you." Stuart glanced at his watch. He motioned toward the table and then looked at Deirdre. "Are you satisfied now that you know my emotional trigger?"

"Yes, I'm satisfied. For now." Deirdre smiled.

"And you? Do you have any or any *other* emotional triggers that you'd like to share with me ... in the interest of safety and solving the case?"

Deirdre glanced down at her manicured nails. She paused and then looked into Stuart's eyes. "Yes, for the record. Prison life doesn't suit me, so let's try to keep our investigation outside of the prison bars from this point forward." She smiled.

Stuart chuckled. "Got it." Stuart held Deirdre's gaze. She liked the way the corners of his eyes crinkled when he smiled.

Stuart cleared his throat, stood and walked toward the table. "Look, I know that we blew it with that extended prison stay, but while Detective Roberts and I were out of town, we did gain some valuable information that may link to the Hayden murder." Stuart reached into a shelf behind the table. "And then there's this." He pulled out a brown envelope, returned to the couch, handed the envelope to Deirdre, and stood in front of her.

"What is it?"

"A brown envelope." He smiled.

"Touché," Deirdre laughed.

"It's the report that I promised you after you were released from the county jail. Plus, it's the copy of that prescription form you asked for ... the one from Charlene Hayden. The Chief also asked me to tell you that we truly appreciate your observations. He thinks the arrest heightened your profile, which may make the real murderer relax and get sloppy." Stuart glanced toward Deirdre's report and the plastic zip-lock bag. "I think that letter in your mailbox is an indication of that."

"Perhaps."

"And there's something else."

Deirdre looked up.

Stuart looked at his watch.

Deirdre's reference to her neighbor reminded him of some added business. "Ah, yes," Stuart walked back to the table, picked up a folder and handed it to Deirdre. "Here's the autopsy report."

Stuart watched as Deirdre studied the report and then looked up at him. "He died between 10 p.m. and 11 p.m.?"

Stuart nodded.

"Traces of Meperidine?"

"That's the drug name. Demerol is its trademark name." Stuart shifted his stance, stepped closer to the couch and sat beside Deirdre.

"Isn't that highly addictive?" She turned toward him.

"Yes, but it's also used commonly in hospitals to relieve patients who are in severe pain. It's a narcotic analgesic." Stuart watched as Deirdre's eyes met his. Her sweet perfume both relaxed and excited him.

"Don't you think it's odd that Jimmy Lee Hayden would have just happened to have this highly addictive prescription drug in his system?"

"It could be odd. Or it could simply be coincidental. We sent for his medical records. A detective in the Narcotics Division is looking into it and will send his report to Captain Brooks, who is very busy, I might add. The Captain will determine its significance. Demerol is a popular street drug, as well as popular prescription drug, so unless we have supporting evidence or start to consider Mrs. Hayden as a serious suspect, my hands are tied." He raised his arms to his waist, palms facing upwards. "This may end up being a cold case."

Deirdre was searching Stuart's expression. He enjoyed being the object of Deirdre's full attention, but he had said enough. Her silence concerned him. "As you journalists might say, the story might be killed. The tape may end up on the cutting room floor, or whatever," he added smartly.

"But don't you think it's odd that this would be considered a cold case so soon?"

"Do you want my professional, or personal, opinion?"

"Both."

"I think it's odd. Frankly, I think it deserves more investigation." He leaned forward.

"Do you think the Captain would have some reason for killing it? Is he trying to cover for–"

"Deirdre," Stuart rubbed his hands on his forehead, "in my line of business, anything is possible."

"So, I may not be off base on this one?" Deirdre scooted forward on the couch and crossed one leg over the other.

"I didn't say that!" Stuart threw his arms out to his sides, acutely aware of her curvaceous calves.

"But you said it's possible."

"Sure, Deirdre, anything is." He clinched his hands into fists and rested them on his lap. "Let's just deal with the facts for now." He moved to the edge of the couch. "We have a murder, a prescription drug form, traces of the drug in the deceased, a nurse as a wife, and some assorted other items, like one of your knives at the crime scene with your fingerprints on it and a piece of jewelry."

"Jewelry? Is that in the report?" Deirdre tightened her grip on the folders.

"Yes, it's all there." Stuart had said enough. He didn't want to reveal too much of what he and Mike discovered in Corpus. He stood and reached into his back pocket, pulled out a business card and handed it to Deirdre. "Here's a different phone number. If you have any information, please call this number, and we'll arrange a place to meet. Okay?"

Stuart watched as Deirdre uncrossed her shapely legs. He leaned forward and offered Deirdre his hand.

Deirdre placed both hands to her side and pushed herself off the couch. "10-4." She smiled.

Stuart followed her to the door.

"Take care, and keep in touch."

CHAPTER TWELVE

Deirdre and CeeCee arranged to meet in the field near the Davis-Scott YMCA directly after an Open House event there. The evening event would draw a multi-racial crowd and some news media, so Deirdre, Curtis and his cameras would draw little attention.

Curtis would be on assignment for the newspaper and take photos of the event and the exchange. Deirdre and Curtis were confident that Victor Reeks would be nearby, if not directly at CeeCee's side.

Deirdre reflected on her earlier conversation with the managing editor, Joe Brown, in his office.

Joe sat at his desk and tapped a pen on the desktop. "Nervous?"

"No more than when I interviewed Henry Kissinger when I was 18," Deirdre shifted in her chair.

Joe laid the pen to rest on some papers on top of his desk. "You don't have to do this. I mean you can back out and I will think no less of you."

"I know. But I'll be fine. It's not like I'm wearing a wire. THAT would make me nervous. Besides, I am sort of looking forward to meeting up with CeeCee. She's ... ummmm ... interesting." Deirdre smiled. "And she's sort of fun to be around. I mean – if I didn't know she was a drug dealer, we might actually be pretty good friends."

"So, you think the drugs are coming from a facility in town?"

"Yes," Deirdre said, as she counted out the details on each finger. "CeeCee made it seem as if they are pure and readily available. I think they are coming directly from none other than Fairlane Hospital. Charlene confirmed with police that the prescription form found at the murder scene was from her pocket. We have the autopsy results." Deirdre dropped her hand. "I need that final tie-in to Charlene, the hospital and the actual murder."

Joe smiled and cocked his head to the side. "Motive?"

"We may not ever know unless we get a confession."

Joe shook his head. "That doesn't seem likely." He crossed his arms. "Do you think the transition is made through security guards at the hospital to the security guards at those apartments?"

Deirdre put her hand to her chin. "I don't know how a security guard would get a hold of drugs." Deirdre dropped her hand. "I have some friends at Fairlane hospital." She raised her eyebrow and smiled. "They are checking things out there."

"So, you've got all the bases covered." Joe clasped his hands together. "After the stuff I've seen in this business over the years, nothing surprises me anymore."

"Ditto on that," Deirdre said as she stood.

"Hey." Joe's gaze met Deirdre's eyes. "Really. Be careful. Okay?"

"Yes. Always."

Maneuvering through traffic near the event brought Deirdre back from her thoughts. She parked at St. Philips College, placed her tiny tape recorder in her pocket and walked toward the Scott-Davis YMCA.

CeeCee's red locks stood out in the crowd. Deirdre saw her and searched to see if CeeCee was with anyone – mainly Victor Reeks. She didn't see him. CeeCee turned and spotted Deirdre. She waved.

Deirdre smiled, waved and picked up her pace. She pressed the "record" button on the recorder in her pocket.

"Hey."

"Hey. The air's a lot fresher here than where we last met."

"*That's* for sure."

"CeeCee, I'm glad you called. We couldn't really talk before, but now we're free."

"Yeah," CeeCee let out a short laugh. "So, you're a big time news reporter, huh?"

"I dunno about big time. But it's a good gig, and it's fun."

"You must be pretty smart. That's what they say about news reporters, ya know. They have the ability to gather a lot of information and filter through it."

"Oh, I don't know about that. I've interviewed a lot of smart people though. And that keeps me on my toes." Deirdre looked past CeeCee and spotted Curtis in the crowd. "I do a lot of research before I meet with them so I can ask intelligent questions." Deirdre smiled and waved her hands in the air, punctuating her words. "That way they don't think I'm an idiot."

"Research." Deirdre felt CeeCee's eyes searching her face. "That sounds like homework."

"Yeah, it is a lot like homework, sort of. But I think it's more fun. I get into something, and then I can spend hours, sometimes all night, researching it."

"A lot of late nights?"

Deirdre paused. She put her hand in her pocket and rested it on her microcassette recorder. "Yeah. It's hard to do, but I pull all-nighters a lot."

"Oh."

"So, CeeCee, what do you do when you're not hanging out at the county jail?"

"Oh, I'm a hairdresser. Part-time. It pays the bills, and, like your job, it's fun. I like making people feel good about how they look."

"Yes, that's quite a talent. I should come to visit you sometime. Do you work weekends?"

"Sometimes. I had to cut back because my wrists started hurting. The docs say it's carpal tunnel syndrome. I don't want an operation."

Deirdre laughed. "There's another thing we have in common, CeeCee. I have carpal tunnel syndrome, too. All that time typing at my keyboard. That's what's doing me in."

CeeCee laughed. Deirdre watched as CeeCee took a long, approving look at her. "Hey, how about that! You know what? I'm going to go get one of my cards from the car. I'd really like you to come visit me at the salon sometime. Maybe even write about it in that newspaper of yours. Do you mind waiting?"

Deirdre nodded and said, "I'll be right here."

CeeCee approached her car and saw Victor leaning on the trunk and taking a drag from his cigarette.

"Are you done?" Victor turned, retrieved the car keys from his pocket and started to walk toward the driver's side of the car.

CeeCee waited until Victor opened the car door and then reached inside. "No, I'm not done," she said as she reached inside for her business card and some other items. She stuffed everything into her jewel-studded wallet.

Victor tapped the top of the car's roof with his keys and stood blocking the open door. CeeCee felt him sizing her up. "Whad'ya mean, you're not done? We gotta go. You said this would only take a second."

CeeCee backed out of the door. She liked the way Victor always wanted to be near her, with her. She liked the way he made her feel wanted, secure.

CeeCee gave Victor a quick kiss on his cheek. "Baby, I'll just be another minute. I'm working on a potential customer here."

Victor grinned and grabbed CeeCee around the waist. "What kind of customer, Baby?"

"Hair customer, of course!" CeeCee smiled and leaned into him. "What did you think?"

"I wasn't sure. You know these uptown gals – sometimes they want much more than a haircut." He brushed his hand through CeeCee's long, red locks.

"Yeah, yeah, yeah." CeeCee lightly patted Victor's cheek with one hand and held the wallet in the other. "But sometimes that is *all* they want."

"All right, then. Have at it. It's good for business." He pulled her towards him, kissed and released her. "I'll be waiting right here."

CeeCee blew Victor a kiss. "Okay, Sweetie." She headed back towards the park and Deirdre.

Victor had warned CeeCee not to get too friendly or generous with that "reporter chick," as he called her. He didn't trust Deirdre ... or anyone, for that matter.

But CeeCee liked Deirdre, and she had a little more than a business card to give her. She had something – in the form of pills – to help ease Deirdre's pain caused by carpal tunnel.

* * *

Letty stabbed into the rich black soil that cradled her flower bed. Nestled in a cozy limestone-edged flower garden, the sweet smell of Jasmine mixed with the crisp scent of the nearby English mint, which served as aromatherapy for Letty's otherwise frazzled nerves.

That woman. Bringing up Captain Brooks. What a Traitor. Cheat. Thief. Maybe she's in grief, but it does not excuse THAT comment. Maybe her husband is better off dead than living with her. I never should have returned that necklace for her. Well, she won't be living in this neighborhood now that she's a single woman.

The sound of Charlene Hayden's and Lucy Mendez's voices sprinkled with an occasional bark from Lucy's dog, Princeton, brought Letty back from her musings.

"Good afternoon," Letty smiled. *That dog better not come near my flower bed. The cost of hauling in this soil is ten times the value of that mutt and I don't want him digging in my flower bed.*

"Princeton," Letty walked to the front of her lawn and grinned through her teeth. "Come here. Let me give you big kisses." Letty deflected the dog from going anywhere near her flower bed by giving him heavy strokes.

Native San Antonio earth was a claylike soil not conducive to growing the variety of flowers that Letty nurtured in her garden.

"Hey, Letty," Lucy stood at the front edge of the flower bed. "These flowers look great. I see you working out here a lot."

"Yes, it's my passion. You know that."

Charlene smirked and shot Letty a sideways glance.

Letty firmly grasped Princeton's collar. "How are you doing, Charlene? Everything going okay?"

Charlene shrugged. "I miss him."

"Sure, Honey. It takes time," Letty gave Princeton a final pat, released him and stood. "Will you be going back to work soon?"

"I have been. I was in last night."

"Oh, well, good for you. Keeping busy is always good medicine."

"Yes, I think so. Actually, Nurse Hutchins called me a few hours ago and asked me to come in a little early tomorrow. So, I'll see her tomorrow evening. Will you be there?"

"No, I was there yesterday morning."

Princeton ran to Lucy and began barking. "Charlene, I'm going to keep walking. Princeton is getting restless."

"Okay, I'll catch up with you." Charlene waved. Letty watched as Lucy walked away.

Letty walked toward Charlene and stood beside her. "I really am sorry about Jimmy Lee."

"Well, he kept nagging me. You know he was onto me. Plus, he wanted to do *more*. That's why I couldn't give you an answer the other day. I need to lay low."

"Well, the hospital has been quite the buzz," Letty whispered. "The patients are complaining that they're in pain."

"Oh." Charlene looked down at the ground and kicked at the grass. She paused, planted her feet firmly, and straightened her shoulders. "Have you talked to Captain Brooks lately?"

"Not to speak of," Letty cleared her throat. "But I hear it may be turned into a cold case soon. Especially since Deirdre has already been in jail once."

Charlene smiled.

Letty felt Charlene's eyes search her face. "I'm glad to hear that, but I'd rather see the evidence against Deirdre stick and see her behind bars again for a very long time."

Letty heard a house door open and slam shut. Footsteps followed. Dave was walking towards her house. She walked closer to her flower bed and signaled for Charlene to do the same.

"Charlene, look at this one." She knelt down close to a Mexican Heather.

Letty knew the discussion had to end. With Dave approaching, ears were all around, and Dave was more of an eavesdropper than he let on to be.

CHAPTER THIRTEEN

Deirdre was calm and in control as soon as she entered the *Daily Sun* building. Something about familiar surroundings gave her a sense of peacefulness. She entered the newsroom and noticed there were several people already gathered in the conference room.

Through the glass walls, Deirdre recognized drug-dealer and CeeCee's boyfriend, Victor Reeks. He stood about 5 feet 6 inches tall. His spindly frame resembled that of a fragile, young evergreen tree that looked as if it could be blown away by a heavy gust of wind. And yet, there was something about him that seemed deeply rooted and securely placed in his surroundings.

Deirdre entered the room and there was a momentary silence as the people in the room stopped to notice her standing in the doorway. Curtis sat on a chair that faced the door near the front of the long conference room table. Managing editor Joe Brown sat across from Curtis with his rounded back towards the door. Deirdre noted Curtis's young and slender face versus Joe's round, full and middle-aged face. Joe was a fatherly type of leader. He was, at times, driving and unrelenting, pushing his staff to leave no stone unturned in an investigation. He required that they visit and revisit sources to verify and confirm facts, quotes and details. Deirdre nodded and gracefully moved towards a chair close to Victor's.

"Victor Reeks, I'd like you to meet one of our top-notch investigative reporters, Deirdre Morgan." Deirdre watched as Joe introduced her to Victor. She made a note to ask Joe about his choice of the words "one of."

As Deirdre extended her right hand to shake Victor's, she glanced up only to catch his deliberate wink at her. It was one of those, "we have a secret" winks. He extended his hand and Deirdre began shaking his cold, sweaty hand. For a brief, fleeting moment, Deirdre had the urge to run out of the conference room. But she knew she was here with a purpose. To find the source of drugs in one of the biggest drug rings in San Antonio.

Victor sat down at the head of the conference room table. He looked relaxed in one of the plush leather chairs, and spoke openly, without giving names or addresses, about the drug operations in the East Side neighborhoods. The newspaper set up the interview by telling Victor that the staff was doing a series on drug trafficking on the streets of San Antonio. There was an agent with the Drug Enforcement Agency posing as a reporter. The agent made the original contact with Victor. He sat at the far end of the conference room table, directly across from Victor. It was a prime spot to observe Victor's actions, facial expressions and, if needed, accost him.

"Oh, man, there's people, ya know, who bring in hundreds of dollars just dealin' pot, and when you get into those crack houses, man, just go up to the door there, or sometimes right out on the sidewalk, man ... act like you're passin' sections of the newspaper or somethin', and you *are* passin' sections of the paper, ya know, but there's a baggie of crack in it," he laughed and with that came a flash of a solid gold tooth that replaced his front, right cuspid. "And those guys bring in thousands a day, ya know. This is big business." Victor paused. Deirdre watched as Victor looked around the room. He looked disappointed that no one seemed impressed.

Deirdre listened and jotted notes. She directed her question to Victor. "Are there certain high-drug seasons? Like times that are busier than others?"

"Naw. This is a daily, hourly, consistent business. Now the supply varies, ya know – who has got what and when it hits the street. But usually there's no problem gettin' the stuff. It's just a matter of makin' a phone call."

"Could you share with us who you make those phone calls to?" Deirdre asked.

"Aw, now, ya know, I'm not gonna give you any names. But I can tell you there's a lotta people into this. A lotta people makin' a profit off o' these drugs. And they all want a piece o' the action."

"Could you be just a little more specific?" Deirdre prodded. "I mean – are they friends of yours or people that you've met over the course of your business dealings? People that you grew up with? I mean, how do you get to know these people?"

Victor smiled and looked Deirdre up and down. "Well, ya know, it takes time. Because there's some trust that goes into these dealin's. And nobody on the streets don't trust nobody. I mean, once you're cleared and they know you ain't gonna skunk on anyone, you can get the goods. But the first time buyin' is always tricky, cuz they wanna make sure you're clean." Victor leaned back in his chair, held his arms to his chest with his elbows pointing outward, and ran his hands down the front of his chest as if to wipe it clean. "No one wants to deal with the copper blood. They're good, but we can usually sniff 'em out. Ya know what I mean?"

Deirdre nodded and wrote "copper" in her notebook then drew an arrow and wrote Stuart at its point.

"C'mon, Victor," the undercover DEA agent addressed him now. "San Antonio's not so cautious are they? I mean, they're dealing with kids on the street, sure. But they're also dealing with businessmen, doctors, lawyers, city leaders, police officers ... the drug folks are pretty well protected."

Deirdre figured that the DEA agent was anxious to get to the video tape. He was leading them right into it, but Deirdre still had a few more questions.

"Victor," Deirdre interrupted.

Victor quickly shifted his pea-like blue eyes towards Deirdre. He had an upwards curl on his lower lip that made him look devious.

"Yes, Ms. Morgan?" his smooth, slithering voice would be soothing if it lacked the undertone of the all-too-apparent hiss.

"Are there suppliers that we haven't considered?" Deirdre shifted in her chair as she tried to weave Victor into an open discussion. "I mean, we know there are drugs supplied from the police, that's just a matter of fact. And drug diversion in the healthcare industry is always a big supplier, but are there other types of sources that we may be missing?"

"What is this?" the DEA agent tossed his pencil onto the table in disgust and leaned back in his chair, folding his arms in front of him.

Victor's eyes shifted quickly between Deirdre and what appeared to be the other reporter. "Yeah ... yeah, sure," Victor said, as he wiped his hands on the tops of his thighs and pulled himself forward on his chair. "There's a lotta supplyin' done through the hospitals, for sure." He paused and crossed his arms across his chest. "The thing is, though, that doctors and nurses ... they don't like to share. They like to keep all the good, pure prescription drugs to themselves. And that's the good stuff."

"Oh," Deirdre replied.

"But that's okay." Victor slapped his hands against the top of his thighs. "We just deal with them differently," he smirked.

"Oh?" Deirdre queried, as she noticed the DEA agent look up, and he pulled his chair forward several inches.

He was writing in his notepad. "How differently?" the DEA agent asked.

Victor fervently plowed his hands through his hair. He cleared his throat. He paused. His voice was barely audible. "Mostly blackmail."

The room was silent.

"Of course," Joe broke the silence. "That's what you use with the politicians and business leaders, too, right?"

"Naw, with them it's just favors. There's always votes, campaign contributions to be had and business deals to bargain for with the politicians. But the good docs and nurses, ya know, sometimes they make mistakes that we learn about, and they don't want lawsuits or media attention. So, sometimes they change a chart here and there or forget to document somethin', and once we get some inside scoop on them, we can pretty much get what we want." He smiled. "And there's usually someone inside ... ya know, a nurse, a doctor, a volunteer, a worker or someone who is an addict. So, we can press them pretty hard. They don't want to lose their jobs, because they need their fix, ya know. So, we can lean on them ..." He paused and made quotes in the air "... to share."

"Hmmmm," the undercover agent was intrigued.

"So, I'm not sure I understand." Deirdre set her pen down and looked at Victor. "If there are all of these tracking systems on drugs, and most of the scripts are now electronic, and some scripts cannot be given out, unless the person getting the prescription shows a picture I.D., so, is it doctors who are the main suppliers?"

"Well ..." Victor paused and shifted in his chair. "May I smoke in here?"

"Sure, go ahead," Joe said. He glanced at the "No Smoking" signs posted around the room.

"That's not exactly the way it is, Deirdre." He pulled out a shiny gold lighter and lit his Marlboro. "It's like this." He inhaled. "We work with whoever needs us. Sometimes they need something from the street; sometimes they need extra cash; and in the doctor's cases, sometimes they just need us to keep somethin' under wraps for them. So we do them a favor, and they do us a favor." Victor leaned back in his chair and looked around the room.

Deirdre handed him an empty soda can. "Here's an ash tray," she smiled.

Victor winked at her. "Thanks."

"What types of drugs are usually supplied through the hospitals?" the DEA agent asked.

"Oh, the usuals – OxyContin, Morphine, Demerol, Valium, Codeine, Lithium ... those are the most popular."

"Are there any hospitals more willing to cooperate?" the DEA agent asked.

"None to speak of," Victor shyly remarked.

"Victor," Joe stood up now, and walked toward the video recorder machine that was set up at the end of the table. "We called you here to find out more about the drug rings in San Antonio. And you've been very helpful thus far. We appreciate that."

Victor nodded and his eyes shifted to the TV screen.

"Now," Joe addressed Victor as if he were his teenage son, "being in a room surrounded by a staff of highly curious and competent investigative reporters and a photographer is quite an intimidating experience. And let me explain why. You see, Victor, they've done their homework. They're aware that you are out – free on the streets – with a pretty serious bond on your head. They also realize that you would do just about anything to maintain your freedom. I'm going to show you something here, Victor, and then we're going to ask you a few more questions. And with your bond in mind, you decide how explicitly you want to answer these questions."

Victor raised his heel and, with the ball of his foot still on the floor, began to shake his leg up and down. He nervously raked his hands through his hair. "Okay, sure." He rubbed the tops of his thighs. "I guess it's show time."

As if on cue, Curtis got up, walked toward the light switch and dimmed the lights. He then hurried to the video recorder and television that were built into the wall at the front of the room and turned them on.

The DVD played the recent events when Victor gave a bag containing a white, powdery substance to Ms. Tyler's assistant in exchange for money. In the next scene, Victor turns around and gave half of the cash to Ricky Barron. The DVD played through to the point of scanning the car that Ms. Tyler's assistant drove away in.

"I told him that was stupid to bring that car," Victor blurted out while watching the scene.

Almost immediately, Curtis leaped up and flashed on the lights.

Joe nodded to Curtis. Then he got up and walked around to where Victor was seated. "Thanks, Curtis." Joe cleared his throat. "Victor, as you can see, we've got a clear and obvious felony here. We can turn it over to the SAPD. But if you'll exchange some names with us and information, we'll let the dust gather on this DVD by placing it in storage ... permanently."

Deirdre hoped Victor would take this deal because she knew that Joe also had photos and transcripts of audio of Deirdre's meeting with CeeCee and a pill exchange there. But she didn't want to use it. Neither did Joe. Those photos and audio were the paper's insurance policy in case they needed to call in another favor.

"Joe," Victor looked him square in the eyes. "If I were to consider giving you any names, I would demand that that DVD be destroyed, not just filed away in storage ... That's the first thing." Victor paused, sat back in his chair and rubbed his chin. "You are asking me to do something that might put my life in danger, so that I can avoid a few months in the slammer ... I mean why would I trust y'all with my life just to save myself from doing time?"

Victor scanned the faces of each person in the room. "No offense to y'all, but really, this is *my life*."

"Because, Victor," Deirdre leaned forward on her chair. "You know that if you were to do some time in the slammer with Councilwoman Tyler knowing of your predicament, she might get a little nervous that you might 'sing' to save your hide. She may decide to take care of you 'from the inside' as they say. She could eliminate any threat to her precious council position by eliminating you. And you know as well as I do that in the state prison system, so-called accidents happen quite frequently."

Victor leaned back in his chair and crossed his hands across his chest. "You don't seem to understand, Deirdre. You see, I'm nothing to the real power on the street. I'm just small potatoes. No one would go through that kinda trouble for me," he answered smugly.

"Really, it wouldn't be any trouble at all," the DEA agent quipped. "Especially if you're small potatoes. That means less inquiries, less questions, less problems." He shifted in his chair and looked down at his notebook. "I used to cover the prisons on my news beat," he added.

Deirdre studied Victor. She wanted the name of the drug connection at Fairlane Hospital, if there was one. Deirdre had been in this business long enough to know that there were few coincidences in this big city. San Antonio was full of criminals, professionals, politicians and police officers knit closely together like a tight-fitting mitten.

Click. Whooooshhhh. Deirdre noticed the humming of the air vent – it was the only sound that filled the otherwise silent room.

"Let's talk." Joe broke the silence. "The *Daily Sun* wants information, and you want freedom and safety, right?" He looked at Victor.

Victor nodded.

"Okay," Joe continued. "We do agree on that." Joe clasped his hands together. Then he spread his hands and dropped them to his sides. "Now, let's talk risk factors, opportunities and mutually beneficial agreements." Joe paused. "The *Daily Sun* stands to gain an exclusive, hard-hitting, probably award-winning investigative series of feature articles. We risk putting all of our eggs in one basket and legal implications by taking Victor's word as the sole truth. For that reason, Victor, we could run the series as a "what if" sort of feature. It would be like the old TV series "Dragnet." Most of you are too young to remember that show, but we could preface the article with," Joe changed his voice to sound like a radio announcer, "What you are about to witness is a real-life scenario, but names and dates have been changed to protect the innocent." Joe smiled.

Everyone in the room chuckled.

Joe paused and then paced across the room and raised his arms. "The risk, of course, for us is being sued. But we have Marcy for that." Joe made a gesture towards Marcy. "The risks for Victor are of him being exposed, and therefore in danger." Joe paused. "We have devised a way so that Victor's identity is kept strictly confidential."

Victor scooted forward in his chair. "There are eyes and ears everywhere. I don't really believe that you can protect my identity, and I'd insist that my lawyer be present at all times."

Joe nodded in agreement. "Okay, let's discuss that. Your lawyer's presence is required, and everyone in this room is sworn to secrecy – complete confidentiality."

Victor scanned the room. "Yeah, right."

Deirdre didn't think he was convinced.

Joe continued. "Victor, even though I trust everyone in this room, I will not discuss the details of how we can keep your name out of this any further if you'll agree to meet with just me, Marcy, and your lawyer."

Victor hung his head and nodded. "Yeah, that sounds good," he muttered.

Joe walked over to Victor and gently put his hand on Victor's shoulder. "Victor, the newspaper has experience in this realm, and we have always been successful with protecting our sources."

Victor looked at Joe. "Okay. Let's do it."

Joe turned to everyone. "Would you all excuse us, please? Victor and Marcy and I need to arrange a meeting."

Deirdre and Curtis walked out of the room in silence. When they reached Deirdre's desk, she turned to Curtis. "It looks like we have it pretty wrapped up."

"Looks that way," Curtis smiled. "So, let's go over the facts." Curtis raised his right hand and began counting by raising each digit, starting with his thumb. "We have our source on the drug tie-in to Councilwoman Tyler."

"Check." Deirdre nodded.

"What about the tie-in to the drugs, the prescription form and the Hayden murder?" Curtis raised his index finger.

"I will get someone in the medical examiner's office to confirm the drug in Hayden's body. And we'll ask the Chief if we can use the information about the prescription form found at the crime scene. We can just report that 'sources confirm' the drugs were the same and leave it at that."

"Okay, check." Curtis raised his next finger, but was distracted by the blinking light on Deirdre's phone. "Someone's calling you." Curtis motioned toward the phone.

"Deirdre Morgan." Pause. "Uh-huhh." Pause. "Curtis is right here." Pause. "Yes, we'll be right there." Deirdre hung up the phone and looked at Curtis. "We've been summoned to Marcy's office."

They turned and walked down the hallway and into Marcy's office.

"Okay," Marcy smiled and waved her arm toward the two chairs in front of her large oak desk. "It looks like we have a deal, and a great story." She was beaming.

"Awesome!" Curtis slapped his hand on his knee.

Deirdre crossed her arms across her chest. "What do you mean 'a deal'?"

"Well, getting the story together. But Joe and I discussed leaving Councilwoman Tyler's involvement out of the initial articles."

Deirdre rolled her eyes and crossed her legs. "What do we gain?"

Marcy raised her hand. "Hear me out."

Joe feels that Advertising and Circulation have finally picked up from East Side businesses and subscriptions have increased. Those departments have worked hard to get to this point ..."

"But ..." Deirdre tried to interrupt.

"You know how the community said that our reporting was biased and coverage for businesses there was barely getting any print? So, we've finally gained their trust again. Joe doesn't feel that it's worth jeopardizing those relations. He said that keeping Tyler out of the articles will make a huge deposit in our bank of favors. Later on, if we need to, we can call in a marker."

Deirdre slammed her palm on Marcy's desk. "So, we just let Tyler walk away scot free? And she makes a big profit on this land deal where the minimum security prison is going to be built? And she continues running drugs through Rightway Security?"

"Not necessarily," Marcy looked at Deirdre in the eyes, and then shifted her attention to Curtis.

"We can still give the information over to the Police Chief." Marcy waved her hands and sat back in her chair. "Let him deal with it. Plus, then we've also made a deposit with the SAPD." Marcy paused and looked at Deirdre. "I know this is against your grain, Deirdre, but if we play nice with the city council and the SAPD, we gain exclusive information before other news outlets."

Curtis piped in, "and we still get the bad guys, Deirdre. If the SAPD does its job right, Tyler will get handcuffs instead of a headline."

"Well, if SAPD moves on Tyler, she'll get headlines, but after her arrest." Marcy added.

Deirdre leaned back in her chair. "Marcy, can I speak with you alone for a minute?"

"Sure." She looked at Curtis, who had already stood.

"I'll get started on the photos," he said, as he walked out of Marcy's office, quietly closing the door behind him.

Deirdre was looking at the photograph on the credenza behind Marcy's desk. It featured Marcy and Marcy's father. *A chip off the ol' block.* Deirdre looked from the photograph to Marcy.

Marcy craned her neck and looked to where Deirdre's eyes had traveled. She turned in her chair and touched the photo frame. "You can't let it go, can you?"

Deirdre uncrossed her arms and legs.

Marcy pulled the photograph closer to her. "My father was a successful, four-term councilman, and yours was just a two-termer."

Deirdre leaned forward in her chair and tinkered with the gold-plated pen and pencil set on Marcy's desk. She picked up the lead crystal paperweight, looked at it and then gingerly placed it back on Marcy's desk.

Marcy looked at Deirdre. "That's it. You think it was about money, don't you?"

"Isn't that how you define success, Marcy? Money? Acquiring things?"

"No, that's not true."

Deirdre looked at her own sensible Timex watch and then looked at Marcy's gold Rolex watch.

"Deirdre, let me tell you something. Shortly after my dad became councilman, my mother was diagnosed with a serious illness, and we had no other health insurance. He had to keep that position to get her the health care she needed." Marcy placed the photo back on its shelf. "Otherwise, we had no medical coverage. It was my mother's life, Deirdre. What would you do?" She turned to look at Deirdre.

Deirdre touched her wristwatch and pulled it down towards her hand. "For twelve years, Marcy? She was ill for twelve years?"

Marcy touched her watch and rubbed her fingers across the crystal-covered face. She turned her chair away from Deirdre and spoke softly. "You get used to certain things, Deirdre."

Deirdre leaned back in her chair and put her palms up, arms open to the side. "Okay, Marcy, we'll do the story your way." Deirdre placed her hands in her lap. "I'll be honest with you, though. I don't like it." She leaned forward in her chair. "Curtis and I still have some work to do. Do you know what the timeline is for the initial articles? My neighborhood is going to be a madhouse when they learn that new evidence points to Charlene Hayden's involvement in her husband's death."

Marcy smiled. "Right. You might want to work on a story out-of-town when this news article breaks." Marcy stood and held out her hand. "Nice job, Deirdre. We've got an award-winner here. Now let's get back to it." She shook Deirdre's hand.

CHAPTER FOURTEEN

Deirdre turned her key in the lock of her home on Kensington Avenue that Friday evening at a quarter past six. She was hot and sweaty – summer had come early to San Antonio – but she was also exhilarated. Cradled in one arm was a little bag with pantyhose and a bottle of "pinkest pink" nail color. She had also packed her microcassette recorder in the bag. Poking out of the top was a magazine with a small invitation to this evening's 50th Anniversary event at Grand Master Kim's Academy. Deirdre had stuffed the invitation into the magazine on her ride home from the local drug store. If she arrived by eight, she'd be there in time for the evening's meal. She glanced at her watch. *Too late to get to the six thirty Black Belt class.*

Deirdre reached inside the door to turn on the front porch light and then walked into the kitchen where she set her few items on the table.

She picked up the bottle of nail polish and felt the smooth, hard glass within her palm. As she rolled it within her hand, she looked up and studied the picture of her and Grand Master In Mook Kim that was hanging on the wall. *Things worth having take time, dedication, hard work and patience.* Deirdre remembered the many hours she had spent over the years in Grand Master Kim's Do Jang, working, sweating, getting it right. Although the physical challenges were grueling, Deirdre enjoyed those as much as she enjoyed applying the mental discipline and tenets of courtesy, integrity, perseverance, self-control and indomitable spirit. As a 2nd Degree Black Belt, she now helped teach the physical and mental aspects of

Tae Kwon Do to new students. Deirdre enjoyed that aspect of her rank.

Her thoughts were interrupted by footsteps, followed by the door opening slightly. Letty poked her head in. She was holding a covered plate in her hands.

"Anybody home?" Letty smiled. "Hey, I brought you some cookies."

Deirdre turned and waved Letty in. "Thanks, Letty! What's the occasion?"

Letty entered the kitchen and pulled up a chair. "I wanted to thank you for making that witness statement about the landscapers." She placed her hands on the table and shuffled the bag and magazine aside. "Your statement helped me get the restraining order in place." She placed her palms across the top of the magazine. "Hey, is this the latest?" She began thumbing through the magazine.

Deirdre took the plate from Letty, uncovered it and set it on the table. She moved the bag of items to the kitchen counter. "Yes, it is. Feel free to look through it." Deirdre glanced at her watch. She reached inside the bag and flipped on the tape recorder. "Hey, is there anything new in the neighborhood? Any new scoops about Jimmy Lee's murder?"

Letty didn't look up from the magazine. "No, not really," She slapped the magazine down on the table and looked up. "Oh, wait! Yes, there is! At the hospital .... The patients. They're complaining about being in pain. Nurse Hutchins and Dr. LeMonroe met about it. And Charlene was called in early to work to meet with Nurse Hutchins. The patients say that the nurses are distributing their medicine, but are they?" Letty raised one eyebrow.

"What does that have to do with Jimmy Lee?"

"Not sure. You're the investigative reporter. I'm just reporting an odd situation. Don't you think it's ... suspicious?"

Deirdre stood and walked to the kitchen cabinets. She reached for and pulled out two plates and two glasses. She placed them on the counter then went to the refrigerator, filled each glass halfway with milk and set them on the table. She returned to the counter for the plates and napkins, grabbed them and set them on the table. Deirdre sat down. She selected a cookie and dunked it in the milk.

Deirdre patted her lips with the napkin. "Letty, these are delicious!"

"Thank you."

"Do you think the nurses are taking the medication? But isn't everything distributed electronically?"

Letty placed her hands on the table. "Yes, and the nurses give the patients the medicine at the time prescribed. However, what if a nurse substituted an aspirin or something that looked like the medicine? Or, if the patient was asleep, and the nurse entered on the report that she had administered the medicine, but really hadn't."

"And you said that Charlene was called in to meet with Nurse Hutchins?"

Letty reached for the glass of milk and took a sip. "Mmmm-Hmmmm."

"And things in the neighborhood. Are they the same?"

Letty put her glass down. "Yes. The same. Charlene is the poor widow, and you're still the one who did it, as far as they're concerned."

"That's crazy." Deirdre gathered her plate and glass, stood and walked toward the kitchen sink.

Letty clasped both hands around her glass. "They just think you're going to get away with it." She reached for another cookie. "Face it, Deirdre. The neighbors resent your success, your youth, your independence. They aren't much different than the deceased Jimmy Lee Hayden."

"But ..." Deirdre raised her hand in protest.

"They resent that you're a Yankee, and your lack of outwardly traditional values, like religion."

"I go to weekly Bible studies ... when I get a chance," Deirdre placed her plate and glass in the sink, then pressed her hands against the cold surface of the kitchen counter.

"But not at *their* church and not with their congregation – so that makes you different."

"Well," Deirdre turned toward Letty and folded her arms in front of her. "I've been friendly, open and honest with them." She shifted her weight and opened her arms. "And I take my relationship with God and Jesus seriously. I'm sure He's trying to teach me a lesson here. I just wish I knew what it is."

"Well ..." Letty placed another cookie on her plate. "Remember when Jesus addressed the Pharisees?"

"When they were trying to trick him?"

Letty snapped her fingers and pointed at Deirdre. "Yes, that part."

"Let them alone; they are blind leaders of the blind, and if the blind lead the blind, both shall fall into the ditch."

Letty took a bite of her cookie and swallowed. "Yep, we're all going into the ditch."

Deirdre shrugged her shoulders. "I sure hope not."

Letty bunched the napkin up and held it to her mouth. "You're pretty confident for an ex-con." She lowered the napkin and placed it on her plate. "As far as I know, you're the only one on the block that's spent time in prison. Hmmm? How about that?"

"That's true. But I was released."

Letty clutched the sides of the plate. "On bond. You're still under the microscope, so I wouldn't get too holier-than-thou."

Deirdre blew out air, shook her head and rolled her eyes toward the ceiling. "Oh, by the way, I'm going to Kim's Anniversary dinner event tonight. So, I've got to start getting ready. It starts at eight."

Letty thumbed through the magazine. "What are you wearing?"

"The black silk dress."

Letty looked up and smiled. "Ohhhh. Nice. Little black dress." She continued scanning the pages. "And the gold charm necklace?"

Deirdre wiped down the counter with a disposable wipe. "Yes." She clicked off the recorder.

"Is Dr. Garrett going to be there? And that handsome Junior Master, Patrick?" Letty held up the magazine. "And can I borrow this until you get back?"

Deirdre tossed the wipe into the garbage. "Yes. Yes and yes."

Letty sucked in a breath of air and released it. "Ohhh, this should be interesting." She blinked. "I wouldn't worry about being late, because you know they'll save you a seat." Letty hesitated. "They'll probably spar over who gets to sit next to you." She batted her eyelids and grinned.

Deirdre crossed her arms. "Very funny." She smiled.

"It's true. They both have the hots for you. I saw it when I went to your first black belt testing." Letty put her hand over her heart and smiled. "They were pining away for you."

Deirdre laughed and started walking toward the table. She made a shooing motion with her hands. "Okay. C'mon, let's go. I gotta get ready."

Letty pushed back in her chair and stood. "Also, when you're done with that new mystery novel you're reading ... the one by that British author, can I borrow it?" Letty began walking toward the door and then looked back at Deirdre. "Please?"

Deirdre started toward the stairs. "Yes, you can borrow the novel."

Letty placed her hand on the doorknob and continued looking at Deirdre. "You will look nice, Deirdre. You always do."

"Thanks."

Letty opened the door. "Okay, I'm leaving. Have fun."

"See ya later. Thanks for the cookies."

Deirdre looked at her watch. Six forty-five.

She turned and hurried up her staircase. "Oh, I better check it out!" Deirdre remembered that her black dress might still be rolled up in a ball on her closet floor. She wore it to a formal dinner event with Dr. Garrett a few weeks ago, was tired when she got home and simply stepped out of her dress. She and Dr. Garrett attended a multiple sclerosis society fundraiser held at San Antonio's downtown Hilton Palacio del

Rio hotel. She and Dr. Garrett were among a small group of couples that "closed-up the place" as Dr. Garrett put it. After leaving the Hilton, three of the couples strolled along the San Antonio Riverwalk. Deirdre remembered what a beautiful night it was. The Riverwalk was always lively, filled with vibrant, happy crowds. Some dined al fresco at well-known restaurants such as Boudro's. Others enjoyed the night life at places like the Hard Rock Café or Howl at the Moon. That evening, Deirdre and Dr. Garrett enjoyed the scenery and their companionship. The reflection of shimmering lights, the amber glow of the full moon and the faint shine from the bright stars reflected on the water that night. As Deirdre reached the top of her staircase, she glanced out the window. The view of the setting sun brought her back from her reminiscing.

She walked into her bedroom and went straight to her walk-in closet. She scanned the floor and then surveyed the area along her built-in closet, then up toward the wooden rods where her formal dresses hung. She spotted the black silk flowing attractively from a padded satin cloth hanger. *Whew!* Deirdre dislodged the dress from its hanger, left her closet and spread the dress gingerly across her bed.

She turned and saw her reflection in the mirror, which set atop her antique dresser nestled against the far wall of her bedroom. She looked to her bathroom door on its left. She grabbed her gun and walked into the bathroom. She placed her gun on the floor beneath the toilet tank and turned on the hot water in the shower. After a quick shower and towel dry, Deirdre applied skin lotion, deodorant and a splash of perfume.

She hurried into her bedroom, opened the antique dresser drawer that held her undergarments, carefully chose some and put them on. She saw her reflection in the mirror and noticed her bare neck, which was in great need of adornment. As she reached for her jewelry box, she noticed the mystery novel which was lying face down and set on a diagonal across the right-hand corner of her dresser.

Deirdre paused. *Strange. I could swear that book was placed squarely on the edge of the dresser, and it was definitely facing up.*

Deirdre's eyes shifted to the jewelry box. The cover was slightly open and the latch was not hooked. She looked from the book to her jewelry box. She took a step backwards.

She backed up to her bed, where she found her purse nearby and reached for her cell phone.

"Detective Beaumont." His soothing voice was a comfort to her.

"I think I need a forensic team here. Now."

"Deirdre? Is that you? I can barely hear you? What did you say?"

Deirdre looked to the jewelry box and then at her clock radio. *7:15 p.m.* "What?" She coughed. Then straightened her shoulders. "Oh, yes. Yes, I'm fine. Must be a bad telephone connection. Hey, I know this is last minute, but do you want to meet for a bite to eat?"

"Sure, what day is good for you?"

"I mean tonight. At eight."

Deirdre waited for what seemed like thirty seconds. "Oh."

"At Kim's Tae Kwon Do on Thousand Oaks and Wetmore."

"Are we working out before dinner?"

Deirdre let out a breath and smiled. "No workout. Just dinner. It's an anniversary event."

"An event. Are you sure –"

Deirdre's words came quickly. "4447 Thousand Oaks, across from the Taco Cabana. Wear a suit. Eight o'clock sharp. I'll see you there."

Deirdre hung up the phone. She took a deep breath, fell to her knees and prayed. "*Lord, why is it so hard for me to fall to my knees? Please forgive me for not turning to You as often as I should, but I need Your help now. You know people's hearts, and I need Your guidance.*"

Deirdre pondered. She knew she could use Letty's relationship with Captain Brooks to make her talk. Evidence was stacking up against Charlene, weakening Charlene's position to blackmail Letty, but Deirdre could pressure Letty to disclose what she might know about Jimmy Lee Hayden's murder.

Deirdre's thoughts were interrupted by a warmth which began in her heart and spread to her shoulders. For some reason, she was prompted to look to her left where a commemorative inscription was listed on a plaque, "Love is Charity in Action."

"*Thank you, Lord.*" Tears fell down Deirdre's cheeks, and she knew how she would approach Letty. Deirdre prayed for a few more minutes. She got up, went to her dresser to apply her makeup, slipped into her dress and shoes, grabbed a matching purse and locked the bedroom door behind her. She secured all of the windows in the house, made sure to set the alarm and secure the doors when she left the house. An overriding sense of calm was within her. She wondered why she was so reluctant to get on her knees and pray. *I need to strengthen my relationship with God. And stop making excuses for things getting in the way of that.*

* * *

Stuart hung up his office phone, glanced at his watch and looked down to inspect his clothes. He wore a shirt, tie and navy blue slacks. *No stains. Not too wrinkled.* He looked up to be sure his sport coat still hung behind his office door. He had just enough time to shower at the office and get to Kim's Tae Kwon Do Academy by eight.

Stuart was glad to spot Deirdre's car in the crowded parking lot at Kim's Academy. When he entered the building, Deirdre was seated at a table for ten, surrounded by eight men and had an open seat to her right.

Stuart walked toward the table. He noticed the way Deirdre's black dress hugged her curves. He watched her sip from a clear plastic cup, engaged in conversation with the muscular man beside her. Deirdre glanced over, recognized Stuart, and placed her cup on the table. With her hand she motioned to Stuart. As he came closer, Deirdre patted the vacant chair. She introduced Stuart as her friend and prospective Tae Kwon Do student.

Throughout dinner, Stuart couldn't help but notice how much Deirdre was admired among the students with whom they shared a table. He watched the way her hands moved when she talked, the way her eyes widened and narrowed as she shared a story. He even admired the fine lines that outlined her lips. During the event, Deirdre was awarded for sharing with others the Tenets of the Academy – courtesy, integrity, perseverance, self-control and indomitable spirit. She accepted the award by downplaying her efforts and giving compliments and thanks to Grand Master Kim, her instructors and fellow students.

With dinner and awards finally over, Deirdre and Stuart had a moment to themselves outside. "So, is there something else we need to do here?"

"Not here." Deirdre turned to look at her car and then looked back to Stuart. Her arm moved quickly as she reached into her purse and pulled out her car keys. "Get in your car and follow me." She hesitated. "I don't mean to be short –"

Stuart rested his hand on Deirdre's shoulder. "Not a problem." With his other hand, Stuart reached into his pocket and jingled his keys. "I'll be right behind you."

She gave her keys a nervous twist. "Let's go."

Upon their arrival at Deirdre's home, she explained to Stuart that her book was turned askew, her jewelry box was not quite closed, and she shared some of Letty's recent comments. Stuart called in an evidence team to get fingerprints of Deirdre's dresser. He also had them place the book, the jewelry box and the glass that Letty drank from into evidence bags and instructed them to make the lab tests a top priority.

As the team dusted for fingerprints, Stuart and Deirdre stood on the front porch.

Stuart quietly addressed Deirdre. "If the prints match, we'll have to question Letty again as to her whereabouts on the night of the murder and on the days that you were in jail – when the letter showed up in your mailbox."

Deirdre clasped her hands together. Stuart watched her for what seemed like minutes. *Silence.* Finally, she said, "I know."

"Have you checked your mail today?" Stuart asked gently.

Deirdre raised her hands in surrender. "No. I was rushing to get to the dinner and ran out of time."

Stuart went inside and selected two pair of latex gloves from the evidence team's bag. He handed Deirdre a pair. "Let's check it now."

Deirdre shined the light from her cell phone onto her mailbox. "Just in case." She handed Stuart her phone light. She reached for the mailbox and pulled on the handle. "Ewww!" She jumped back.

Stuart lunged forward to catch the bundle falling out of Deirdre's mailbox. Deirdre stooped down to catch her cell phone before it landed on the driveway. Deirdre felt the warmth of Stuart's powerful arms against hers just before they tumbled onto the edge of her front lawn.

Prone on his back with Deirdre cradled in his right arm, Stuart held up the bundle with his left hand. "Flowers," he whispered. "Looks like dark, black roses."

It was dark. Deirdre closed her eyes and absorbed the wonderful contrast of Stuart's light spicy scent against his muscular body. She lay there pressed against him.

Charlene Hayden's porch light switched on.

Deirdre quickly rolled away from Stuart and got back onto her feet. "There's a card."

"Let's take this inside." Stuart pressed his right hand onto the ground, holding the bouquet of flowers upright as he rose to his feet.

Once inside, Deirdre and Stuart opened the envelope. The card read "MURDERER." The handwriting was similar to that on the white envelope of the letter left in the mailbox.

Deirdre watched as Stuart inspected each carefully. He placed them in an evidence bag, marked them and handed the flower and card to his team for testing.

CHAPTER FIFTEEN

Charlene fumbled for the switch to her front porch light. Her finger twitched involuntarily as it groped then found the edge of the switch. *Off.* Charlene felt her chest tightening and her heart racing as she strained to see out her small front-door window. Deirdre and a man were tumbling on Deirdre's front lawn. The man held a bundle of flowers in the air.

"Deirdre got her delivery," Charlene sneered.

Charlene backed away from her front door window, sucked in air and stood frozen in her dimly lit hallway. The faint glow illuminating from the tiny arms of her wristwatch, beckoned. *10:35 p.m.* "Time to go to work."

Charlene arrived a few minutes early for her night shift at Fairlane Hospital. On her way to the central nurses' station, she paused in the hallway in front of Nurse Hutchins' office. The shutters were closed and traces of light spilled through the door. Charlene crept nearer to the door, pressing her ear closer. Within the office were muffled sounds of a man's voice.

Hmmm. Dr. LeMonroe. She heard footsteps draw nearer, so she hustled to the central nurses' station.

* * *

Dr. LeMonroe and Nurse Hutchins studied the timeline they'd drawn out on the whiteboard in Nurse Hutchins' office. They'd been investigating this, on and off, for a few weeks. Finally, at 10 p.m. this Friday evening, they had a good summary of events.

"There are only three nurses who administer meds to those patients," Dr. LeMonroe walked towards the whiteboard and pointed to a group of names.

Nurse Hutchins was seated at her desk. She straightened her shoulders and took a deep breath.

"Yes, and now for the moment of truth." She cleared her throat. "Security e-mailed me clips from the surveillance cameras."

Dr. LeMonroe turned toward Nurse Hutchins, walked to her desk and stood behind her chair. "All right, then ..." he said.

Nurse Hutchins clicked her mouse, opening the file. "There it is," Nurse Hutchins reached for her pen and wrote 12:01 a.m. on her notepad.

They watched the scene unfold. Charlene slipped into Room 309 with a small white cup, typical for holding meds. Noticing that the patient's eyes were closed, she reached into her pocket, slipped out two similar looking pills, placed them on his tray while she poured the pills from within the cup, into her palm and then slid those into her pocket.

"Well, there it is," said Dr. LeMonroe. "I knew it was worth putting those extra cameras in the rooms. And the Human Resources department fought us on that." He lightly tapped the computer screen. "But there you have it. Those cameras have paid off already."

Nurse Hutchins positioned her pen squarely in the middle of the notepad and leaned back into her chair. "Wow. I would have never suspected Charlene Hayden of such a thing."

Dr. LeMonroe's eyes moved to the clock. "Shift starts in five minutes."

Nurse Hutchins straightened her spine, moved forward and planted her feet on the floor. She picked up a paperbound file from her desk, and fanned through its pages.

"These are all of the reports. They confirm that Charlene was keeping the prescribed Demerol and giving the patients something else."

Dr. LeMonroe shifted his stance. "Mmm-Hmmm." He rested his hand on the back of Nurse Hutchins chair. "You okay?"

"Sure." Nurse Hutchins' face softened, and she placed her hand over Dr. LeMonroe's. "You know what I say, 'When employees make choices, they must live with the consequences.'"

Nurse Hutchins faced Dr. LeMonroe. She noticed how the unruly strands of his brown hair nestled comfortably on his forehead. "Thanks for your help on this."

He smiled. "No problem." He paused and moved his free hand to emphasize his words. "I care about these patients." Dr. LeMonroe's blue eyes glistened like diamond chips on the water. He sighed as if in surrender and sifted strands of his chestnut brown hair through his manicured hand. "I wouldn't have stayed in school for nearly 30 years, with more than a decade of that earning little money, getting little rest and garnering little gratitude, if I weren't dedicated to caring about these folks." He shook his head. "And – something just didn't seem right. They were not sleeping well and that impedes the healing process." He met Nurse Hutchins' gaze as he rested his hand on top of hers and slightly squeezed it. "And I do care about how the added stress might affect you. You're a great charge nurse. We don't want to lose you." His eyes met Nurse Hutchins' and held.

She blushed, turned her head, slowly retrieved her hand and made a deliberate motion pulling up her left wrist – a platform for her modern wristwatch – toward her chest. "A manager from Personnel is scheduled to meet me here in ..." She outlined the face of the glass timepiece between her right thumb and index finger. "... fifteen minutes." Nurse Hutchins pushed back in her chair to stand. "Thank you again."

Dr. LeMonroe took a step back and nodded. "Any time. Just call any time." He turned toward the door and began to exit. He turned slightly, "Besides, I prescribed many of those medicines. I feel responsible for them being administered correctly."

She smiled. "As do I."

He paused, "You *are* what I wish all nurses were."

"Thanks." Nurse Hutchins neatly lined up the file folders into a pile on her desk, held them upright, tapping them firmly. She prepared for the upcoming meeting with Charlene Hayden.

* * *

Charlene swung the door open to Nurse Hutchins' office with a firm push. Enough to make a statement but not provoke a reprimand. The smell of antiseptic consumed her. The sterile surroundings twisted at her insides. A flush of cold air blew from the registers overhead, sending a slight chill through her.

Her eyes were drawn to a square table in the center of the room, host to Nurse Hutchins and a woman dressed in business casual attire. The hue of the fluorescent lights cast eerie shadows across their faces. It unnerved her, like a frightened school girl who'd been caught smoking in the bathroom.

"Good evening, Charlene," Nurse Hutchins motioned to a chair. "Please have a seat. I believe you've met Ms. Reynolds."

Charlene made her way to the table, pausing only to shoot a glance at the folders assembled there. As she approached, she recognized Ms. Reynolds. "Yes, we've met at training classes."

"How are you doing this evening?" Nurse Hutchins sounded concerned.

"Fine," Charlene postured herself neatly into a chair and pulled it close to the table.

Nurse Hutchins gave Charlene an apprehensive smile. "Remember when I asked if you needed more time off to grieve your husband's tragic, tragic death?" she asked.

"Yes." Charlene drew her hands into a prayerful pose in front of her chest. "May he rest in peace." She feigned sympathy.

A bit of small talk ensued, Charlene answered tentatively at first, but then loosened up.

This isn't so bad. I might just get through this. She paused and relaxed, pushing back in her chair.

"Nurse Hutchins, I'm sure you have a lot to do, and that you and Ms. Reynolds didn't call me in for small talk." Charlene looked at Ms. Reynolds and then to Nurse Hutchins. She fidgeted with the edge of her shirt sleeve. "What's on your mind? I don't mean to be rude, but I have patients waiting.

And they've already been complaining of pain and seem restless."

"Well, that's what we wanted to talk about."

Charlene noticed as Nurse Hutchins furrowed her brow and squared her shoulders.

"Charlene, we've been doing some investigation into the recent patient unrest, and we are presented with some disturbing facts. Facts that under best circumstances require you to be placed on temporary suspension, and at worst lead to criminal charges and possible prosecution." Charlene watched as Nurse Hutchins firmly placed her hand on top of the folder. "Charlene, you seem like a smart person." Charlene nodded in agreement. "You have a lot going for you. It's a shame to see you in a situation like this. So, we'd like to know if someone is putting you up to certain actions that we're about to review." Nurse Hutchins' eyes softened. She relaxed her shoulders and leaned in toward Charlene. "Maybe you could help us, and then maybe we could help you."

Charlene wedged the ball of her right foot into her ankle. She reached for a strand of hair and began twisting it, leaning her elbow on top of the table. She drew her other hand to her chin, her index finger covering her lips.

"I can understand if you're nervous," Nurse Hutchins feigned sympathy. "Texas is not exactly lenient when it comes to drug diversion."

Charlene's eyes widened. "What? What do you mean?"

"We have video of you switching medications in patients' rooms; we have charts of you dispensing extra Demerol, and that's just the beginning."

Charlene's jaw dropped. She quickly recoiled, licking her lips. "You mentioned helping you." Charlene felt the nervous tick in her right shoulder, causing it to rise involuntarily. "With what?"

"Names, places –"

Charlene expelled a puff of air. "You want names?" Charlene breathed quickly now. "I can give you some names." Charlene wiped her hand across her forehead, and then cradled her head in both hands. She began massaging her temples methodically, as if to rid herself of something within. "My late husband, for one. He was the connection." Charlene rubbed her forehead fervently as she looked down at the table." I was just the supplier. He kept pressuring me." Charlene looked up to meet Nurse Hutchins' gaze. "The real bad guys, the ones you want, they're in much higher places, councilmen, policemen, even a female Judge. It goes much higher. They were just using me."

Charlene watched as Ms. Reynolds picked up her pen. Charlene's words came quickly now as she talked to Nurse Hutchins.

Ms. Reynolds wrote everything down: names, dates, phone numbers. Charlene even provided names of other suppliers within the hospital system. She mentioned city council members, police officers, and high-profile members of the community.

Charlene took a breath. She was relieved, nearly exhilarated to be informing Nurse Hutchins and Ms. Reynolds. "And there's a Judge, Judge Janet Longfellow. She presides at many drug-related cases. At some point in the proceedings, the Judge orders the evidence to be taken to her chambers. That's when she switches out the cocaine with a different powder, marijuana for oregano. There is no court reporter, and no record, and often not even the attorneys are present. She confiscates some really good street drugs. That's how my husband got the idea for me to do the same ... to switch out prescription drugs with something else."

Charlene sighed a breath of relief. She was beaming now, looked relieved and nodded as if seeking approval from Nurse Hutchins and Ms. Reynolds.

Charlene noticed that with this latest revelation, Ms. Reynolds, who was writing almost frantically, paused and looked up at Nurse Hutchins. Almost in unison, each of their jaws dropped.

Charlene voluntarily signed a 90-day suspension form. The reason listed was extended time for mental health and grief.

Charlene left and passed through the hallway. She was half expecting to be escorted out of Nurse Hutchins' office, but hers were the only footsteps along the tiled floor.

Although relieved that her calm exterior did not arouse suspicions, Charlene was seething.

She left the hospital, but did not go straight home. Charlene stopped at the butcher shop to purchase an expensive cut of kobe-style beef. *This will seal the fate of Deirdre Morgan*, she plotted.

CHAPTER SIXTEEN

The phone rang early, awaking Deirdre. She met Curtis and together they went to meet with CeeCee, who said that Victor was acting strange and took off for Corpus Christi early this morning.

CeeCee and Deirdre had breakfast in a small, family-owned café on the East Side of San Antonio. Curtis picked the spot, then excused himself from breakfast. Deirdre noticed that he left in the car for about 30 minutes and then returned.

The door squealed, announcing Curtis' return to the diner. Then it shut behind him with a loud snap, as if to emphasize his arrival. Deirdre scraped up the last bite of her scrambled eggs and motioned to CeeCee who was taking her last swallow of coffee.

"Deirdre," Curtis said with a mysterious gleam in his eye. He anxiously twirled the car keys around his index finger. Deirdre found the random *swoosh – clank* of the keys relaxing. Her eyes met Curtis'. He placed the keys in his pocket and looked from Deirdre to CeeCee.

"Oh, umm, I apologize for leaving like that, but we got a call and we need to get to the office."

Deirdre and CeeCee said their goodbyes and made vague references to a next get-together. Then Curtis drove Deirdre to the office.

On the way to the office, Curtis shared where he had actually gone.

"Deirdre, I gotta tell you something." Deirdre noted the excitement in his voice. He hardly kept both hands on the steering wheel. "While you were there with CeeCee, I went for a little jaunt around the neighborhood – you know that's Councilwoman Tyler's side of town."

Deirdre nodded.

"I drove by her council office, then by her house. And, then by her brother's house, and guess who was walkin' out the door?" He didn't wait for a response. "And I took photos of it all. I took photos of it all!"

"Please don't do a Victory dance while you're driving." Deirdre smiled and grabbed onto the steering wheel.

"Did you hear what I said though?" He flicked her hand off the wheel. "We have photos of the car, with the license plate and the one and only Victor Reeks and Ricky Barron and the Security Director from Rightway Security coming out of her house."

Deirdre interrupted. "CeeCee said Victor was headed to Corpus Christi this morning."

Deirdre worked her jaw back and forth for a moment. "Are you sure it was the guy from Rightway Security?"

Curtis pressed the brake, jerking Deirdre and him forward a little, as he stopped at a traffic light. Curtis shot her a glance. "Yes. Absolutely." The light turned green. Curtis accelerated slowly. "Interesting, right?"

* * *

The message light on Deirdre's desk phone was blinking. It was from the police crime lab. Detective Beaumont had asked them to call her with fingerprint identification results, and if she would call them back as soon as possible.

She returned the call. "This is Deirdre Morgan."

"Oh, yes," the voice on the other end was that of what sounded like a young woman. "One moment. I'll get Officer Neill."

"Neill here."

"This is Deirdre Morgan. You left me a message to call ASAP."

"Yes, Miss Morgan. I have instructions from Detective Beaumont to give you a message." Deirdre heard papers shuffling on the other end of the telephone line. "Oh, yes, here it is." He paused. "Lab results confirm your suspicions. Letty's prints. All of them."

"And is there more?"

"No, ma'am, that's it." Deirdre waited. "He's been real busy today. He got in early, and jetted right back out on some urgent matters. I think out of town."

Deirdre made a mental note. "Thank you, Officer Neill." Deirdre's voice mellowed. "Thank you very much. I'm going to be working on some things today for an article I'm writing. Will you be in the lab today all day?"

"Yes, ma'am. You can reach me at this number. Just ask for me and I'll drop whatever I'm doin', and I'll try to answer any questions you might have."

"Thank you, Officer Neill. Goodbye."

Deirdre hung up the phone. "Beaumont's out of town, too." Her heart was racing. "And those were Letty's prints on my jewelry box and necklace and letters." She blurted.

Their eyes locked.

"Let's go."

They rushed to Curtis' car and drove to Deirdre's house.

Twenty minutes after leaving the office, Deirdre and Curtis pulled around the street corner leading to her home. Curtis decelerated after the turn, noticing that a fire truck and many of her neighbors were gathered in front of and on Letty's front lawn.

"What in the world?" Deirdre spoke aloud.

Within seconds of pulling into her driveway, Deirdre caught sight of her neighbor Dave in her rearview mirror. His polo shirt was untucked, one of his pant legs was stuck inside of his cowboy boot, while the other hung flat over his other boot. Dave darted towards Deirdre.

"You'd better come quick." Dave's eyes jabbed at Deirdre. "Letty's pretty shakin' up."

"Wha—?"

"Princeton – Lucy's dog." Dave's arms were flailing. "We think he's dead . . . on Letty's front lawn!"

Deirdre blinked. She looked up and down the street and noticed a black Cadillac pulling away from the front of Charlene's house. She looked at her watch. *1:22 p.m.*

Deirdre saw that Letty and Lucy Menendez were kneeling in front of Princeton. Letty's arms cradled around Lucy's neck as they rocked back and forth methodically.

Deirdre froze. She noticed one of her earrings nestled into the mulchy, hollow ground near Princeton's limp body.

Before Deirdre could react, she heard the quick thump of heavy footsteps beside her. Lucy's husband hustled Deirdre out of the way, nearly pushing her to the ground as he reached for and caressed Lucy.

He hugged Lucy as he raised her to her feet. "Está bien. Está bien. They'll care for him. They'll care for him."

Just then a fireman saw the glistening jewel, and plucked it up with a gloved hand.

Deirdre noticed Letty staring at Princeton, then Letty met Deirdre's gaze. Her eyes narrowed to slits. Letty approached Deirdre, her breath heated. "Where have you been this morning, Deirdre Morgan? I hope you have a good explanation, because you're the only one who could've done this."

Deirdre blinked and took a step back. "Letty, why, I don't believe you just said that!" Deirdre reached for Letty's hand, but Letty pulled away.

Deirdre stepped closer. "Why don't you come join me for a cup of coffee or tea, and we can discuss just what is going on."

"Fine." Her words spit out like fire from a dragon's mouth. "Right now. But, I'm getting my puppy dog. He is staying right beside me."

"That's fine with me," said Deirdre.

Moments later, Letty and her new puppy were in Deirdre's kitchen. Deirdre had set her microcassette recorder inside of a kitchen drawer, well within range of their conversation.

Dave was nowhere in sight. Curtis lingered on Deirdre's front porch.

"Okay, Letty. What gives?" Deirdre asked.

"Well, I got home from my volunteer shift, and came home to a dog passed out on my front lawn. I thought he'd gotten into my plants, and I was livid. As I got closer, I noticed that he wasn't moving.

"I touched him and no movement, nothing. I felt for a pulse. Just then Lucy was out searching for Princeton, and I hollered to her 'Hey, over here!' I had my cell phone in my pocket, so I dialed 9-1-1, thinking they might be able to revive Princeton, but I don't think so. I'm pretty sure he's dead."

"From what? Are your plants poisonous?"

"Nope. Not at all. No oleanders, nothing toxic." Letty continued. "So how do you explain that? Then, when the fireman moved him, they saw a slab of beef underneath Princeton. They are sending it in for testing, but they said it looks like Princeton was drugged."

Deirdre let out a breath. "That's ridiculous! Why would anyone harm Princeton, or any dog, for that matter?"

"Just to be cruel, Deirdre." Letty's eyes accused. "Why would anyone murder Jimmy Lee Hayden? Just to be cruel, to prove a point, whatever." Her voice sounded wire tight. Letty held the cup of coffee to her forehead letting the warm surface soothe her.

"And where have *you* been?" You left out of here pretty early, and I heard cars going back and forth, up and down this street early this morning. Before I left for the hospital."

"Letty," Deirdre's tender look embraced Letty's hardened features. "This morning at about 7:30, Curtis picked me up and we went out for breakfast. Then we went to my office, where we confirmed that your fingerprints were all over items in my mailbox, my bedroom, and specifically my jewelry box. So what gives?"

Letty crossed her arms across her chest. "I don't know what you're talking about. And that sounds preposterous. I've been in your house lots of times." Letty slapped her hands on the table, "Hey, who was even looking for my fingerprints, and why?"

"Letty, there's evidence that you and Charlene are involved with some pretty heavy drug trafficking, and that is what led to Jimmy Lee's death."

Letty slammed her hands on the table and shot up from her seat. She darted towards her dog, who was barking and scratching at Deirdre's sliding glass door, overlooking Deirdre's backyard.

"You have some nerve, Deirdre Morgan!" Letty struggled with the lock on Deirdre's back door, "You are the main suspect." Letty's voice rose urgently, like a battle cry, as she overcame the door's lock. "Don't you think I saw that earring on my front lawn? I believe it is one of yours."

The dog sprinted towards the hedge bordering Charlene Hayden's home. Deirdre worried that his incessant barking would muffle her tape recording.

"I understand that you are all too familiar with my jewelry box, Letty, but I have done nothing wrong, so I am not worried." Deirdre felt amazingly calm, despite what appeared to be newly planted evidence.

Thank you, God. I know You're here.

Deirdre's face flooded with empathy. She leaned closer to Letty. "I can help you." Deirdre felt the confident thumping of her heart. "I know you wouldn't do such a thing."

Letty lowered her head. "I was just being nice." She pushed her hand across her brow, forcing her hair back so hard it must have hurt. "Charlene asked me to deliver a package. That was all I did. I didn't know what was in the package." Letty's eyes were pleading. "Next thing I know. Charlene shows me photographs of me delivering the package to who she claims is an undercover agent in the Narcotics Division." Letty shook her head. "I'm in these photos ... with him and some Captain someone named Brooks ... and they are not very flattering to me. It even looks like I'm making advances towards the Captain – so a drug dealer and a woman of loose morals." Letty slumped her shoulders. "Really, Deirdre. You gotta believe me. I was just tryin' to be nice. And Charlene, well, she took my niceness as a weakness, and boy did she take advantage of that." Letty seemed guarded. "And now ... Now, I'm in it up to my eyeballs, as they say." Letty lifted her head, looking straight ahead. She paused. "Charlene says she'll make sure I take the blame for all of it." Letty raised her voice urgently. She turned towards the back sliding glass door.

Letty sprang to her feet as she watched her dog break through Deirdre's hedge, heading towards Charlene's house ... "GET BACK HERE!" Letty darted towards Charlene Hayden's home in pursuit of her puppy.

Deirdre stayed close behind.

"Letty, what are you –"

Charlene stepped out of her back door. Deirdre felt a cold chill take ahold of her shoulders and travel quickly throughout her body.

Charlene greeted Letty and Deirdre in her backyard as they struggled to gain control of Letty's dog.

"Your puppy having a hard time?" Charlene's words seeped through the warm, humid Texas air. "I'd be freaked out too if a neighborhood dog died on my front lawn." Charlene clutched her arms like a woman on a chilly night.

"Charlene," Letty butted in. "What time did you get home? I didn't see you at Fairlane Hospital this morning." Letty's voice was tense.

Charlene's stare was cold, her words warm. Her smile was too wide and long to be taken seriously. "I was not feeling well. So, I left early." She cleared her throat. "I'm heading down to Corpus Christi to relax. My friend lent me her place to stay." She shifted her weight.

The dead silence collided with the puppy's persistent playfulness. Charlene's voice cut through the stillness. "Hey, do you want to put your puppy in my garage, and we can go inside to share a cup of coffee?" She licked her lips. "I haven't really visited with y'all lately. Maybe it's time." Charlene's voice trailed off.

Letty's puppy frolicked between Deirdre's feet. "I'll put him in the garage," Deirdre volunteered. She hoped to snatch a few moments alone to dash back to her house and get her cell phone.

"I'll help you put the puppy in the garage, Deirdre." As Charlene approached the dog, Deirdre dropped back. Her heart was racing, a shrill voice screaming in her head.

"Letty, do you want to start the coffee?" Charlene's voice punctured Deirdre's despair. "Deirdre and I will be there in a minute."

Filled now with terror, Deirdre scooped up the dog and headed toward the garage. Charlene was talking, but Deirdre didn't hear anything. A sense of panic surged within her chest. She glanced at her watch. 3:33.

She remembered John 3:33: *"Those who believe Jesus discover that God is a fountain of truth."*

"Truth," Deirdre thought. "I hope Letty will let it prevail."

* * *

Charlene had thoughts for one thing. *Revenge*. She waited until Deirdre entered the garage, then she struck with all of her strength. Deirdre hit the ground harder than she had thought. The indoor-outdoor carpet cushioned her fall with a definitive splat on the concrete floor.

Charlene scrambled to get some rope – a bungee cord would have to do. She grasped Deirdre's arms and secured them tightly behind her back.

Reaching into her pocket, Charlene produced a Lithium capsule and slipped it under Deirdre's tongue.

A chamois served nicely as a gag.

Shoving Deirdre into her car, she locked the doors. She couldn't risk starting the car for fear Letty might hear. She'd save that treat for later. The thought of watching Deirdre slip into a cold, fatal sleep excited her.

She pushed back Deirdre's eyelids, ensuring she was not conscious, and felt her pulse. Barely there, but alive.

The puppy whimpered. "Aagggh," Charlene seized the dog in disgust and carried it into the kitchen.

Inside, Letty was setting three coffee cups on the table, the solid sound of ceramic cups clinking against the glass-top table was accompanied by the bubbling gust of the coffee percolator.

"Deirdre had to go home for a bit. She got an urgent call," Charlene lied.

"Oh." Letty poured Charlene a cup of coffee. "I'll wait for her here." Letty poured coffee into her own cup. "We should talk."

* * *

Struggling against the throbbing pain, Deirdre opened her eyes slowly. A trace of light slipped in, casting frightening shadows throughout the car. She thrust her tongue enough to push the capsule beneath it into the thick material wedged into her mouth.

Deirdre listened for any hint of Charlene's presence. Silence. She thought of Letty and her puppy and ached to help them.

A whisper of self-preservation gripped her groggy mind. She willed her body to move, slightly at first. Slumped sideways across the front seat, she rolled onto her back wincing at the stabbing pain across her skull. *Dear Lord.*

Ignoring the pain, Deirdre planted her feet firmly against the passenger car door. Deirdre pushed, sliding her body across the front seat, closer to the steering wheel. As she moved, she felt something warm dripping down the back of her neck. Closing her eyes and straining against exhaustion, she arched her back and placed her feet against the seat, pushing down as she slid her shoulders across the front seat. Trembling, she prayed for the pain to subside. Using her legs to drive her body upward, she sat in front of the steering wheel. Her vision blurred, her world was spinning.

In a final guttural blow of exertion, Deirdre drove her head into the car horn on the steering wheel.

* * *

Inside Charlene's kitchen, Letty jumped to her feet. "What is that noise?"

"Oh, must be that stray cat again," Charlene had to act quickly. "Sometimes it gets into my garage, jumps in the window and messes with the car."

"Let's go see," Letty started toward the door.

Charlene grabbed Letty's arm. "Why don't we just wait for Deirdre. She should be here soon."

"She'll find us," Letty left the kitchen and headed towards the garage.

"Wait!" Charlene cried, chasing after her. "I can ..." Letty walked into the garage.

"Explain." Charlene caught up to Letty, who had a horrified look on her face.

* * *

Letty saw Deirdre's body curled over the steering wheel inside of Charlene's car.

"DEIRDRE!" Letty rushed to the car.

Charlene's hot breath slithered down the back of Letty's neck. "Leave her alone!"

Letty opened the car door and caught Deirdre's limp body as it tumbled into her. Letty prayed to God for strength.

Terrifed, Letty turned to see the madness screaming in Charlene's eyes. Charlene's arms were raised overhead. Letty bent over Deirdre's body, letting her back absorb Charlene's blow, which was obstructed by the open car door.

Letty pushed her body into the car door, knocking it back and Charlene against the wall.

Charlene let out a muffled cry.

Letty pushed Deirdre's body back into the car, slid into the front seat beside her, closed and locked the doors.

Charlene stood frozen against the wall. "It's complicated Letty." Her eyes became slits. "But you will pay for this." She lunged forward.

Trembling, Letty did all she could, which was to put the car in Neutral, letting it roll back into the garage door. Then she lunged forward into the car's horn.

Charlene cried in agony, covering her ears.

"Okay, STOP!" She screamed. "I CAN'T TAKE IT! You know what I did!" Tears flowed freely now. "You know what I had to do!" Her body slumped to the ground.

Letty heard Curtis and Dave banging on the outside of the garage door. Trembling, she pressed harder into the car's horn.

Moments later, Letty heard sirens blaring. The high, whistling sound contrasted greatly with Charlene's low, deep sobs.

* * *

Deirdre had no idea where she was or how long she had been asleep. When she opened her eyes, she saw the blur of a female silhouette. Deirdre's mouth was dry and she was overwhelmed by the smell of hospital-grade antiseptics mixed with the more pleasant aroma of turkey and mashed potatoes.

She winced at the pounding in her head. She tried to sit up.

"You're awake," Letty turned and rushed to stand beside her. "Just in time for lunch." She smiled and nodded toward the food tray.

"What happened?" Delicate feelings of anxiety sifted through her mind.

"You're okay now." Letty patted her hand.

"Charlene knocked you out, then slipped you some drugs." Letty flitted at a stray strand of brown hair upon her brow. "But it's all over now. She confessed and is wearing a nice orange suit in the County Jail, awaiting bail hearing." She paused and smiled. "You know how that is."

Letty reached for a newspaper lying on the bedside table. "And look here." She pointed to the newspaper. "Your handsome Detective Beaumont made a major drug bust in Corpus Christi while you were sleeping in Charlene's car."

Deirdre smiled. Closed her eyes and leaned back.

Thank you, God.

A tear hung on the edge of Deirdre's right eyelid.

"All in His time. Right, Letty? All in His time." She drifted back to a sweet, peaceful sleep.

CHAPTER SEVENTEEN

The folded newspaper taunted him. Stuart stared at its ragged edges violating the wooden boundaries of his inbox.

The sharp edges are defined by a heavy steel blade, which scrapes against its metal guide as its weight bears down on the newspaper, making precise cuts on each 16-page news spread.

The hot Ginseng tea was a welcome, secure comfort compared to the unknown on the front page of the newspaper.

He didn't take his eyes off of it.

If he didn't look soon, Mike would be in his office telling him about the front-page news, and he didn't want that. He wanted it in black and white, and on his terms. He needed this to be private. All of his life, he'd been a silent observer of the way things played out in the media.

He'd been at plenty of high-powered political events where people's careers were made or broken. He'd sat in many courtrooms where he witnessed the injustices within the justice system. He'd waited silently in chambers, where he observed the back-stabbing at the county commissioner and city council meetings.

Back then, Stuart watched how his father meticulously vetted information until he thought he'd grasped the true story – then, and only then, was it ready to publish.

His dad had news rules:

1. Statement of facts had to be substantiated by at least two sources.

2. Ideas had to be presented with at least one opposing point of view.

3. Press releases had to be vetted through an opposing source, researched and substantiated.

4. Get it right the first time so there are no regrets.

"Everyone has their perception of the truth," his dad would say. "A newspaper has the responsibility to gather those perceptions, research and investigate the facts ..."

"I thought the truth was black and white." Stuart said.

"No, son, only the black ink on white paper is that simple."

"And what about your opinions?"

"That's editorial and belongs on the Editorial page," his dad would wave his hand, as if to dismiss the editorials. "There's no place for one's opinion in the news. Just the facts. The plain and simple truth, which is plainly not so simple to uncover."

"Hmmph," Stuart shrugged, as the memory faded.

The facts. That's what I need to see right now. The facts, and how Deirdre may have used them and me for her personal gain.

Stuart reached for the newspaper. Other than a short article about a business event, Deirdre Morgan had no bylines.

"Ahem." Stuart looked up to see Mike entering his office. He had a bundle of papers underneath his right arm. "Good morning, L.G."

"What do you have there?"

"Oh, a newspaper or two."

"I have the *Daily Sun* right here, and there's nothing about the Hayden murder."

Mike was grinning like a Cheshire Cat. "I know."

Stuart crossed his arms. "Okay, hand it over."

Mike walked to Stuart's desk and slapped the *San Antonio Current,* an alternative San Antonio newspaper, into Stuart's chest.

The front-page photo featured a photo of Charlene Hayden with the headline: "Why'd She Do It?" Stuart flipped to the front-page and began reading.

"Sources disclosed that Hayden had become addicted to prescription opiates supplied to him by his wife, a nurse. When she tried to cut him off, he threatened to go to the police with all of Charlene's secrets – which allegedly were many.

"Charged with drug diversion, the source alleges that Charlene Hayden was the main source for an active drug trafficking ring on San Antonio's East Side with a possible tie-in to a drug ring in Corpus Christi."

Stuart lowered the newspaper and looked at Mike. "Possible tie-in to Corpus Christi?" He raised one brow. "Why is this in the *Current*? What about the *Daily Sun*? Morgan's award-winning article? Her plaque on the wall?"

"Seems like she got scooped."

"Do you really believe that, Mike?"

Mike wrinkled his brow. "No." He paused. "Why don't you give her a call?"

Stuart folded the newspaper and then rested it on his desk.

"You two sure became chummy during this whole Jimmy Lee Hayden ordeal," Mike teased.

Stuart clasped his hands together and placed them on the newspaper. "The case is solved. I don't have a valid business reason to call her."

"Who said anything about business?" Mike shrugged and smiled, leaving Stuart alone.

When you're raised in the lap of a news editor, you're fated to be a skeptic. To seek out, whether it exists or not, the other side of the story. The facts that are buried in the story's final paragraph that often get cut out altogether. The omission of pertinent facts. The context of each misplaced quote. All newspapers read like a supermarket tabloid. Objectivity is as much a fantasy as a news reporter with integrity who is determined to seek the truth. This Deirdre Morgan would take some getting used to.

* * *

The restaurant Stuart chose as their meeting spot was dimly lit and had a quiet, intimate ambiance. Their chairs were nestled dangerously close to each other's.

"Scooped?" Deirdre pressed her hand against Stuart's shoulder. Her eyes smiled. "Do you really believe that I got scooped?" Deirdre clicked her glass of sparkling white grape juice against Stuart's water glasses."

"Well, it sure does look that way." He smiled.

"Don't believe everything you see, Detective Beaumont." Her lips glistened against the sparkling juice. "The world is not black and white."

"My world is."

"Not even *I* believe that."

"So what is the scoop? And how did you put it all together?" Stuart asked.

"True to her form, Marcy didn't want to splash the truth about our East Side politician and her highbrow friends on the front page or any page of the *Daily Sun*. I gave her my word that I would honor her wishes. I also gave Joe a few words. I told him that to preserve my integrity as a journalist, I could not be forced to compromise the coverage. It would reflect poorly on me and the paper. It was better to let it go."

"I see, but how did you put it together? And how did it end up in the *Current*?"

"As an astute detective, like you, knows, money, addictions and love interests make strange bedfellows and can turn friends into strangers – and sometimes enemies." Deirdre leaned back in her chair.

Stuart leaned forward in his chair. "Friends?"

"Letty, my neighbor." Deirdre leaned forward and placed her hands on the table.

"She confessed everything. How she was helping Charlene frame me, and was able to get Grand Master Kim to give her another gold charm necklace explaining that she'd lost mine and then returned the new one to my jewelry box. Letty also explained the strange things happening at the hospital – patients complaining of pain, despite being administered their medications, and the ensuing investigation by Nurse Hutchins and Dr. LeMonroe that led to Charlene's suspension and eventual arrest. Of course, I had all of this conversation with Letty on tape."

"I know. Information from that tape was helpful in getting Charlene to talk after we arrested her and questioned her about the narcotics incident at the hospital." Stuart moved his hands closer to Deirdre's. "Jimmy Lee was really pressuring Charlene to divert more drugs from the hospital. He was expanding his 'business' to Corpus Christi. He had even enrolled in a program to become a phlebotomist, so that he could work in a hospital, too. Finally, he put too much pressure on Charlene. She committed that gruesome murder before she left for work that night. She drugged his wine. He was out cold by the time she stabbed him."

Stuart touched Deirdre's hand. "But *why* did Letty help Charlene frame *you*? And how did you get Letty to talk?"

Deirdre liked the feel of his strong, warm hand against hers. She glanced sideways and pressed her other hand against her cold glass. "Letty's motives are too complicated to go into." Deirdre released the grip on her glass. "I appealed to her through love." Deirdre looked to the right, then ran the fingers of her free hand through her dusty blonde hair. "Then Letty saw Charlene for who she is, and she, well," Deirdre twirled her hair within her fingers. "She saved me from Charlene." Deirdre's eyes softened. "Letty's had a tough time, but she's a good person. I reminded her that living a lie would have far-reaching consequences. That was enough for her." Deirdre paused and smiled. "But I did have a plan B, in case appealing to her conscience didn't work."

Stuart leaned back. "Right. Always good to have a backup, but I'm surprised you didn't need to use it." He shifted forward again.

"Sometimes light in a sea of darkness is all it takes."

Stuart shook his head and looked down. "Rarely. And how did the news story end up in the *Current*?"

Deirdre took a breath. "Curtis and I just happened to be talking about the case at Dough restaurant. We left our table to watch the chef cook. When we returned to our table, our notes, tapes and photographs were gone. We made a police report – plus our recording equipment was stolen."

"Really?" Stuart displayed a half grin. The rich, deep chocolate of his eyes were filled with amusement.

"Yes. Of course, we had to report it." She held out her hand as if it were a matter of fact.

"So, who would do such a thing? I mean stealing notebooks, photographs and recorders? What were they thinking? What were they after?"

"A good news story, of course." Deirdre placed her other hand close to Stuart's.

"Of course. That's all you journalists ever want." He moved to caress her other hand.

Deirdre pulled one hand away and pointed her index finger toward the sky. "Correction, Detective Beaumont. *Amateur* journalists want a good news story." Deirdre rested her hand on top of Stuart's. "The pursuit of a good news story above all else and at the detriment of compromising one's values is the goal of an *amateur* journalist. Or a broadcast journalist – one whose primary goal is to satisfy his or her ego. But the *professional*, Mr. Beaumont," She leaned in toward Stuart. "the *professional* is a journalist of substance." She noticed Stuart roll his eyes as he smiled.

Stuart cleared his throat and moved his chair closer to Deirdre's. "How does one define a journalist of substance?"

Deirdre felt his lips close to hers. She paused. "A journalist of substance is one who believes in ..." Stuart leaned in closer. Deirdre's eyes were locked on his. Her words came out slowly, "the power of the pen to ..." She felt his warm, moist lips against hers, and she surrendered to the moment. She leaned back and took a deep breath and tried to concentrate on her words, which came out slowly. "to ... serve up justice, not power." She sighed and returned for another kiss. She felt his strong body against hers and was glad the business part of their relationship was over.

Stuart leaned his head back. "Oh, did I mention that there's another investigation the Chief wants you to look into?"

Deirdre nuzzled her head into Stuart's chest. "No, you didn't mention it."

"A close friend of his family was found dead in the Arnot river."

Deirdre quickly pulled back. "In Florence? Italy?"

Stuart nodded. "Yes, that's the one."

"When do we start the investigation?"

Stuart studied his watch. His grip tightened around Deirdre's waist. "Not tonight, Deirdre. Tomorrow."

Other Titles from Parson Place Press

For more information regarding discounts, see www.parsonplacepress.com/store

Digital Evangelism: You Can Do It, Too!

By Michael L. White

ISBN 13: 978-0-9842163-2-1

Add digital evangelism to your repertoire of ministry skills

A Time For Everything: the Kevin Zimmerman Story (Second Edition)

by Michael L. White

ISBN 13: 978-0-9842163-6-9

Does God still work miracles today as He did in the Bible?

From Slave to Governor: the Unlikely Life of Lott Cary

By Perry Thomas

ISBN 13: 978-0-9786567-9-9

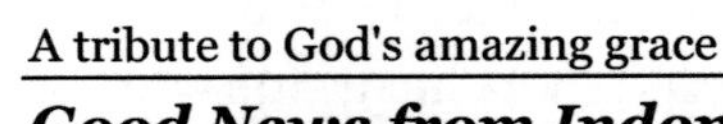

A tribute to God's amazing grace

Good News from Indonesia: Heartwarming Stories from the Land of the Tsunami

by Perry Thomas

ISBN 13: 978-0- 9842163-4-5

Your vicarious missionary experience begins here

Other Titles
from Parson Place Press

For more information regarding discounts, see
www.parsonplacepress.com/store

The Robins of St. Lawrence Church

Story and Full-color Illustrations by Amy Dyas

ISBN 13: 978-0-9786567-8-2

Take off on this high-flying adventure

Seasons of the Heart

by Lori Stratton

ISBN 13: 978-0-9786567-2-0

Let your heart be stirred anew

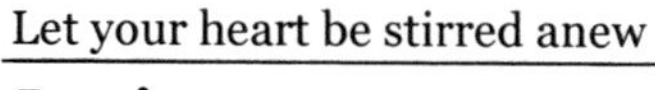

Louisa

by Richard Emmel

ISBN 13: 978-0-9786567-3-7

Based on the life of American poet, Phillis Wheatley

The Resource Book for Louisa: A Guide for Teachers

by Gena McReynolds and Richard Emmel

ISBN 13: 978-0-9786567-5-1

For elementary and middle school teachers

CPSIA information can be obtained at www.ICGtesting.com
Printed in the USA
LVOW121519050712

288897LV00015B/121/P